WRECKER

IRON ROGUES MC

FIONA DAVENPORT

WRECKER

After discovering corruption by a real estate developer, Peyton Carr got caught in a building collapse. Now the biker who rescued her won't let her out of his sight.

Reid "Wrecker" Owens was used to pulling people from the rubble, but saving Peyton once wasn't enough. Not when she was still in danger. Wrecker's instincts were on high alert, and anyone who came for Peyton would have to go through him first.

1

WRECKER

The mansion where we'd just broken up a voyeurism and human trafficking ring smelled like sweat and blood. I needed some fucking air, so I stepped outside with Maverick, the vice president of the Iron Rogues, the motorcycle club I was patched into.

Some of my club brothers had already cleared out and were riding back to Old Bridge, where our compound was located. Others had stayed behind to transport the women we'd pulled from the basement or handle the bastards who'd paid to watch or buy them. They'd been locked in a reinforced viewing room while two of our guys, Storm and Racer, were taking their sweet time making sure they got a proper welcome to hell.

I stood outside on the gravel, my boots planted wide and my jaw tight. A thin breeze rustled through the trees behind the house, tugging mist around the edges of the property. The night air was cool, but my leather cut still stuck to my back, soaked with sweat and fury that hadn't burned off.

Maverick stood nearby, his eyes scanning the road as headlights bounced along the driveway— associates from allied clubs finally rolling in to help clean up what we'd unearthed. We didn't need them for the violence. But we'd need them to finish burying this nightmare in a way that stuck.

He lifted a hand to wave one crew in, then turned slightly toward me. "You staying or heading back with the others?"

Before I could answer, my burner buzzed in my cut. Not my club phone but the one I kept for work. The one no one called unless shit had hit the fan somewhere it shouldn't have.

I dug it out and squinted at the screen. Chris Kelley. A name I hadn't seen in over a year. We met when I worked as a Combat Engineer and EOD (Explosive Ordnance Disposal) tech for Army Special Operations.

"Gimme a sec," I muttered, already walking toward the edge of the driveway.

I answered with a simple, "Yeah?"

A gruff chuckle rolled through the line, scratchy and weathered. "Still answering the same way, I see."

"And you still only call when something's on fire," I shot back.

"I didn't want to bother the firefighters. Figured I'd call the wrecking ball instead."

I grunted, leaning back against the cold brick behind me. "You ever think about calling just to grab a drink? Or is kicking down walls still our love language? I swear, one day, you're gonna call me just to talk and give me a fucking heart attack."

"You'd hate me if I called just to catch up."

"I already hate you," I said dryly.

"Don't get all sentimental on me now." He chuckled again, but the humor faded fast. "I need your help. I need eyes that don't belong to a city payroll. Someone who can read a footprint in a pile of rubble. Who's blown up more buildings than he's walked through."

That snapped my spine a little straighter. "This about those buildings in Nashville?"

"Not just Nashville," Kelley said. "We've had seven collapses in three months, stretching from there down to Chattanooga. No common thread. No identical blueprints. No pattern we can pin.

Different builders. Different ages. The timing's off. The materials shouldn't be failing at the rate they are."

My hand gripped the phone a little tighter. "Shit. Anyone dead?"

"Not yet. But it's only luck keeping the body count low."

"And you think it's sabotage," I said flatly.

"I'm pretty damn sure at least one of them was a blast job. Tight. Clean. Directional as hell. You ever see a load-bearing wall sheer off like a fuckin' jigsaw? 'Cause I hadn't. Not before last week."

The air felt heavier suddenly, thick with pressure. I didn't often get a call before a structure was destroyed. Usually, I was brought in to safely dismantle or clear debris from collapsed buildings to execute rescue efforts. Especially if they needed someone to blow through to get to survivors.

"I'll bite," I muttered. "Why me?"

Kelley sighed. "Because I can't trust the city engineers, and you don't answer to anyone. I need this quiet, off the record. Just eyes and instincts."

I ran a hand down my face. "You got any ideas on where the next site is?"

"Wouldn't be calling you if I didn't." I heard

paper rustling, then he continued. "There's a garage in downtown Chattanooga. Six stories. Load zones have shifted without explanation. Reinforced beams showing signs of early fatigue. Unstable core."

"Good target, but tell me why you think it might be next."

"There's something else," Kelley admitted.

"I fucking hope so. Or you'll be sending me on a wild goose chase, and I might not answer the next time you call."

"Bullshit. You answer every damn time. That's how I know I'm special."

"Nah. That's just how you know I'm not smart enough to block your number."

Kelley barked a laugh. "Missed you too, man. Anyway, a woman's been poking around each of the demo sites. Requests inspection records. Blueprints. Sometimes she flashes a student ID and sometimes a city permit. We thought she was local news at first, but she doesn't ask the right questions for a journalist. We got eyes on her anyway. Turns out, she visited the last site a week before the building collapsed."

"Think she's involved?"

"Maybe. Maybe not. But she's connected somehow. I'm texting you her info along with the address of the parking garage. I'll email you everything else we've collected on the situation."

I glanced around at the shit show we were still cleaning up. "You need me to go there now?"

"I don't think there's any need to go right this minute. Besides, don't you live like over an hour from Chattanooga? It's the fucking ass crack of dawn."

"More reason to go now. I'm over two hours away," I grunted.

"You're in Nashville?"

"Yeah. Dealing with club shit."

A second later, my phone buzzed. One image. I didn't see anything else.

I opened it without thinking—and then fucking stopped breathing.

The photo wasn't much. A snapshot taken from a distance, but it was sharp, making it easy to pick out the details. But even through the pixel haze, she was...gorgeous. Black curls tumbled down her back in a riot of soft chaos. Her skin had a warm glow, her jaw was tight with focus, and she was squinting at a set of blueprints like they'd personally insulted her. Long legs in fitted jeans, safety vest flung open, clipboard balanced on one hip.

But what stopped me cold were her eyes.

Even in low res, I could tell they were violet.

Who the fuck had eyes like that?

My dick woke up like it had been shot full of adrenaline. The damn thing hadn't twitched for a woman in longer than I wanted to admit. But now it roared to life.

Heat spiked low in my gut, fierce and instinctive. I didn't know her name yet—but I already knew she was mine.

"What's her name?" I asked, voice rougher than I wanted.

"Peyton Carr. Twenty. Civil engineering student. Finishing up her junior year. We thought she was just nosy, but now I'm not so sure."

I let the silence stretch for a second, still staring at her photo.

"Reid?" Kelley prompted.

"I'm on it," I muttered. "Send me the garage specs. And the collapse reports."

"You still got access to your old blast modeling shit?"

"You think I'd ever throw that out?"

He snorted. "Didn't figure. Call me if you find anything."

The line went dead.

I just stood there for a minute, phone still glowing in my hand, her photo burning into my brain.

Maverick's voice cut in behind me. "That your rescue bat-signal phone?"

I didn't look up. "Something like that."

He wandered closer. "You okay?"

I didn't answer.

He stepped up to my side, and I glanced up to see him staring at the screen. Saw her picture. And the way I was looking at it. *Fuck.*

His mouth curled into a shit-eating grin. "You better not be falling for a woman off a damn photo."

"Don't," I growled.

Maverick laughed, full-bodied and wicked. "Oh, this is gonna be fun. You gave Hawk so much hell for that shit."

"Fuck off."

"I'm just sayin'. She's cute. Real sweet lookin'. Might even like you back, once she gets past your resting murder face."

I glared at him, but it didn't land.

He just slapped me on the back. "Go handle your shit, brother."

I shoved my phone back in my pocket and

stalked toward my bike. The night was thick and still, but the pulse in my throat was rapid.

I didn't know what I'd find.

Didn't know if she was part of the problem or the key to the truth.

But after I checked out this site, I was gonna find her and figure it out.

2

PEYTON

"Tell me again why you're doing this so early on a Saturday morning instead of sleeping in like a normal college student?"

I rolled my eyes at my roommate as I shoved an infrared camera into my backpack and zipped it shut. "Because I want to be employed after graduation."

Jennifer leaned against the doorframe of our bathroom, arms crossed over her chest. "How many times do I need to remind you that you're not even a senior yet?"

"As often as I have to explain that it hasn't stopped me from being obsessed with my capstone project already." I tucked my phone into the back pocket of my jeans before glancing up at her. "I'm telling you, something suspicious is going on here. These collapses can't be random."

She gave me a familiar look. One that made it clear she was equal parts amused and concerned. "You sound like one of those true crime podcasters who think everything is a conspiracy."

"And look how many cold cases have been solved because they can't stop digging into them," I pointed out.

Jennifer shook her head with an exasperated sigh. "And you're off to investigate alone. What happened to centering your project around peer-reviewed research? Or even just field work that doesn't require you to traipse around buildings that could be falling apart, for all you know?"

I paused in front of the mirror to pull my hair into a low ponytail. "I just want to check the parking garage out and compare it to the blueprints and inspection records I pulled. I'll be in and out in thirty minutes."

She arched her brow. "That's what everyone says before they wind up dead and featured on a crime podcast."

"Thanks for being so supportive," I muttered, ducking past her to go into my room and grab the spiral notebook off my desk.

I was old-school when it came to taking notes, a habit I learned from my dad. A big part of me wished I could text him right now. He would've loved this project.

Heck, he probably would've driven me there himself just to talk me through what to look for...and ended up inside the parking garage with me because he couldn't resist taking a look for himself.

Instead, I had to settle for doing it on my own and hoping that he was looking down on me and knew I was trying to make him proud.

"Fine, but you better text me updates." She grabbed a pillow from my bed and tossed it at me.

"Deal." I caught the pillow midair and sent it sailing straight back to her.

Jennifer's laughter trailed me as I left, making me smile as I headed to my car.

It took me a little more than half an hour to drive to the building I wanted to check out, as it was located in Chattanooga, a few towns away from our college campus. The five-level reinforced concrete garage had probably been approved to support the three-story office building a few blocks down the street since they'd been built around the same time.

Since I wanted to walk the perimeter first, I left my car around the corner where parallel parking was allowed. Slinging my backpack over one shoulder, I crossed the street, my eyes narrowing when I got close to the garage. The plans I'd found said it was finished a few years ago, but there was already significant spalling on the concrete along the base. Rust stains bled through areas they shouldn't have, indicating potential issues with waterproofing. I also found honeycombing that was deeper than 25 mm in the concrete, which made me worry even more about the building's structural integrity.

Discovering this many visible issues during a simple walk around the garage left me wondering how it had passed inspections during construction. I pulled out my phone and began snapping pictures, ensuring I captured multiple angles. The entrance ramp led to the first level, which was mostly empty. I glanced around and made my way to the far stairwell. The elevator was taped off, which didn't surprise me. Most of the lights worked, but one flickered overhead as I descended to the lower level.

I didn't have to explore the basement level for long before I discovered a steel stress fracture. It had already been sealed, but whoever was responsible for the repair had done a sloppy job. This just raised even more red flags.

It was too soon in the parking garage's lifespan

for this kind of damage, especially when it was designed to bear heavier loads. Either the steel was lower grade than what had been approved, or someone had cut corners. Big ones.

A chill crept up the back of my neck, raising goose bumps under my jacket. I stood slowly and tucked my infrared camera into my backpack, but something about the floor caught my eye. I crouched down to examine a sunken concrete slab.

As I ran my fingers lightly across the jagged outline where the concrete had settled unevenly, I shook my head with a deep sigh. Spotting exposed rebar above my head, my concern deepened even more.

I rose slowly, sweeping my flashlight across the far wall. The beam of light hit more issues. Too many for a relatively new structure since parking garages typically had a minimum lifespan of thirty years. Major repairs shouldn't be needed for at least ten years.

None of this made sense unless the builder did more than cut a few corners. They had to be down-right negligent.

Just as I reached for my notebook to jot down a few thoughts, a loud pop echoed through the garage.

My head snapped up.

The noise came again, louder this time. Then it was followed by a deep groan.

I stepped back from the beam instinctively, my heart thudding. "No, no, no..."

There was a sharp crack, followed by a deep rumble that rolled beneath my feet.

Instinct kicked in hard. I needed to get somewhere safer than the middle of the basement floor of a five-story parking garage if it was about to tumble down around me.

I bolted for the stairwell I'd used to get down here, adrenaline surging through me as I sprinted faster than I'd ever gone before.

The concrete around me shuddered. A chunk of ceiling collapsed behind me with a deafening crash. Dust exploded into the air, blinding me for a second, but I didn't stop.

I couldn't if I wanted any hope of getting out of here alive.

My backpack slammed against my side as I pushed harder, barely dodging another slab that fell from the wall. Screaming filled my ears, and I didn't realize the sound was coming from me until I was inches from the stairwell door.

I dove, and the world around me exploded.

I hit the ground hard, banging my head. But that

didn't stop me from bracing against the rectangular frame while pain lanced through my shoulder. It was the safest place to be as chunks of concrete and steel crashed around me.

"Please, please, please," I chanted, squeezing my eyes shut.

I thought about my dad and hoped he was truly watching over me so my mom wouldn't get a call telling her I was gone.

When the worst of it passed, everything was dim. Dust filled the air, making it hard to breathe. It was so thick that I couldn't see anything. Not that it mattered since there was nowhere for me to go.

My hand fumbled for my phone in my pocket, but it did me no good because the screen was too badly cracked to use it.

I wasn't sure how long I was there, alone in the darkness and debris, before I finally heard sirens far above me.

I yelled until my throat was sore, but nobody came.

Drifting in and out of awareness, I finally heard a deep voice barking orders.

"Help!" I screamed as loudly as I could. "I'm over here! Please, help me!"

"Silence," the man roared. "I think I heard her."

"You did," I squeaked, my voice giving out at the very worst time possible.

Refusing to give up, I tapped my broken phone against the doorframe, tears streaming down my cheeks. It seemed like hours later when broad hands cleared debris to my left as though it was nothing.

All I could see of my rescuer was that he was big and fierce.

He shouted something I couldn't make out, and then his eyes locked on mine.

They were sharp. Fierce. Full of fury.

I wasn't alone.

Relief washed over me so hard I almost sobbed.

Then everything went black.

3

WRECKER

I was halfway into the Chattanooga city limits when the blast lit up the sky. Fire bloomed in the distance—red and orange licking up into the purple and pink hues of the sunrise.

A minute later, I could see the garage—blown apart like a fucking matchbox. Concrete and steel skeletons shearing sideways. Sirens already screamed in the distance.

Fuck. I was too late.

My gut dropped.

There was no reason to believe that Peyton had been there when the building blew, but something inside me shouted to get there as fast as possible.

The sun had barely clawed its way above the skyline, but the air was already thick with smoke.

The wreckage smoked heavily, and ash floated in lazy spirals through the morning light. Sirens wailed down side streets, and radio static cracked over handhelds. I pulled up slow, cutting the Harley's engine.

Her car was here.

Around the corner from the garage, like it had every damn right to be there, parallel-parked tight and precise. There wasn't a scratch on it, and the sight of the untouched vehicle made my stomach turn because that meant she'd still been inside when the building gave out.

"Fuck," I growled under my breath, swinging off the bike.

My boots hit pavement hard as I stalked toward the barricade line, weaving between orange cones and yellow tape, and pushing past a huddle of EMTs who instinctively stepped aside. Bodie, the fire chief, spotted me, squinted against the smoke, and then let out a breath like he'd probably been holding it since the blast.

A police rookie stepped in front of me with his version of an authoritative expression.

"Sir, you can't be here. Go back behind the barricade."

I was about to tear the little shit a new one, but the chief jogged over and tapped the kid on the shoulder. "I wouldn't piss off the demolition expert, boot. I suggest you get to know our allies so you don't insult another one."

The kid's eyes went wide, then he nodded and scurried away.

"Wrecker," Bodie greeted with a grim smile as he shook my hand. "Damn good timing."

"Wish I'd beat the fucking fireworks," I muttered, scanning the scene. "Garage go fast or slow?"

"Fast. Chain reaction. Whole west side collapsed within seconds."

"And the girl?"

He looked surprised for a moment, then shook it off. He'd worked with me long enough to know I had other sources and often knew shit before they did.

He nodded grimly. "A witness across the street saw her go in before the blast. She hasn't come out. Fire's nearly extinguished. We were just about to start working our way in."

"Don't," I snapped, cutting him a sharp look. "I'll take it from here."

"You want command?" he offered.

"You're damn right I do."

One of the reasons I liked working with Bodie was because we never had a pissing match over who was in charge. He handled the flames, but no one was better at entry and rescue efforts than me.

Bodie spun to his men. "New orders—follow the man with the death stare. He says jump, you ask how high, midair."

That got me a few side-eyes from any guys I didn't recognize, but no one argued.

Satisfied, I nodded. I didn't have time for explanations or any other bullshit. I was already moving as I grabbed the pair of gloves Bodie was holding out and snapped them on. I barked out instructions—starting with the hoses to suppress the smoke and ash that was clogging the air, obstructing our vision and making it difficult to breathe. "Need two crews to start stabilizing the corner frame, another two on standby with portable jacks."

I knew where she'd entered, thanks to the witness. That narrowed the search zone.

But every second ticked louder. My heart pounded in fear and anticipation.

Inside the structure, the light was uneven—blinding shafts of sun cut through broken levels, but everything else was dipped in shadow. Dust choked the air, settling on my cut, sticking to the sweat already gathering at the base of my neck. The whole damn place felt like a fucking coffin with the lid just waiting to be slammed closed. Steel twisted overhead, groaning as it settled.

I didn't flinch. I'd worked in tighter, hotter, and more fucked-up conditions.

Didn't mean I wasn't silently flipping my shit.

She was in here somewhere. And I had no idea if I would be able to find her in time. I could already be too late.

Just like—*No. Not fucking going there. Not now.*

"Talk to me," I barked to the nearest firefighter.

"There could be a partial void in the northeast stairwell. A small air pocket. If she got there in time, she might..." He broke off when he clocked my thunderous expression. "We found a break in the lower slab, could be that the area would be accessible through it."

"Show me."

Best-case scenario was getting to Peyton without additional explosives. I was the fucking best at my job, but there was always an added risk, and I couldn't stomach the idea of putting Peyton in any more danger.

He led the way, and I followed, every step heavier than the last. We ran into crumbled concrete and jagged rebar, creating a wall.

"Fuck," the guy muttered. "The place is still deteriorating."

Even with the level of this explosion, the building shouldn't have been falling apart this fast and with such extensive damage. I filed that away to examine after I got Peyton to safety.

Another firefighter appeared with a K12 saw and handed it to me. Carefully, I cleared the wall, and my flashlight swept the interior as we climbed through the opening.

"There." I pointed at a narrow gap between support beams.

And then I heard a voice—tired and scared, but still somehow sexy as hell. *For fuck's sake, Wrecker. Get your head in the fucking game!*

Following the sound as we called back and forth, I finally saw movement.

Barely visible. But it was there.

A flicker of a hand. A glint of something metallic —phone maybe. Tapping.

Smart girl.

She was giving me a precise location so I was careful not to clear the debris in the wrong spot and cause her little nook to cave in. I felt a streak of pride when I realized she'd braced herself in the doorframe.

"Found her," I shouted, dropping to my knees.

There was slight movement again, then my eyes locked with hers, and feelings I didn't recognize slammed into me. Knowing I didn't have time to dwell on that shit, I broke our gazes and began barking orders. "We need to clear this section over here, then I'll be able to wedge through."

Several hands joined me, and I directed which pieces of the wreckage needed to be cleared out of our path. As we moved the steel and concrete, my scowl intensified at the evidence that pointed at low-grade materials that should have been caught during inspection. Something was definitely off, but my focus needed to be on the rescue.

It wasn't long before the opening was big enough for me to scrape through. "Gotta bring her back up," I called. "Get me a ladder and a wider exit."

My elbows ground against the debris and the fine grime that coated everything, even my throat and lungs.

When my boots thumped on the ground, I swept out my flashlight once more, and the beam of my light hit her face.

Peyton.

She looked like an angel dragged through hell. Blood streaked across one temple, her curls were wild and matted, and gray powder coated her, even her lashes. Slumped in the stairwell frame, she was wedged tight, one arm looped over her ribs like she'd been trying to protect herself.

Her chest was rising—barely.

I got to her seconds before she sagged into unconsciousness. My arm shot out, bracing her head from the jagged metal behind her. My heart thundered so loud, I couldn't hear the rest of the crew anymore.

"I have you," I muttered, low and rough, my voice cracking in my throat. "You're in my arms now, baby."

She winced even though she was unconscious when I shifted her. I glanced down to assess where else she might be injured, cringing when I got a good look at her shoulder. Her jacket was torn at the seam, bunched awkwardly where she'd landed, and the skin beneath was already starting to mottle—an angry bloom of deep red and purple spreading along the curve of her shoulder.

It looked raw and swollen as if the muscle underneath had taken the brunt of the impact. Blood vessels had burst in uneven streaks, and the entire area was starting to swell. It looked tender and appeared hot, even from a few inches away.

She'd be sore as hell for a couple of days. But Blade could give her pain meds that would keep her shoulder functional while it healed, so long as she hadn't broken anything.

I clenched my jaw so hard it clicked. Someone was gonna pay for putting her through this.

The wreckage shifted again with a long groan, and I jumped into action. I cleared debris around her with brute force—chunks of concrete, bent steel—tossing everything out of my way. When she was free, I scooped her up like she weighed nothing.

Her body curled into me on instinct, one hand—luckily her good one—fisting in my shirt even though she was unconscious.

Something inside me cracked and welded shut at the same time.

I just knew. She was everything to me now. Mine.

She was soft in my arms but full of grit. Her jeans were torn, her jacket half-burned along the sleeve, but her skin was warm against mine. And her sweet, earthy scent, faint with sweat and fear, hit me like a punch to the gut. That same dark heat from before surged low in my belly, rage and lust twining in a twisted knot.

Even battered and bruised, she was the most beautiful thing I'd ever seen.

Fucking hell, I wanted to bury myself deep inside her until the world faded away.

But first, I had to get us both the fuck out of here and make sure she would be okay.

I retraced the few steps I'd taken and grunted in approval when I reached the ladder they'd lowered into the hole. Holding her firmly, while also being as gentle as possible, I slowly climbed up to the surface.

Bodie's face appeared, and he reached his hands down, expecting me to transfer Peyton into his arms. I growled deep in my chest, and his eyes grew wide before he nodded and backed up. Near the top, I took his outstretched hand to help me clear the last few rungs.

"Gotta go, Wrecker," he said urgently. "I don't know how long the rest of the structure will hold."

More sirens howled outside as I carried her clear of the building. An EMT lunged forward to help, reaching for her.

I bared my teeth. "Touch her and lose your fucking hand."

The guy backed off so fast he tripped over his own boots. *Smart move, asshole.*

"She's hurt," Bodie said, carefully moving to

stand next to me. "We need to get her to the hospital."

"No," I rasped, my voice scratchy from inhaling all the dust, and the tightness in my chest because Peyton still hadn't woken up. "*You* don't."

His brows drew together. "You can't keep her from medical—"

"She'll get medical," I grunted. "But not at some random hospital. This is Iron Rogues business."

That shut him up.

I didn't know for sure if Peyton had been targeted, but my instincts were rarely, if ever, wrong. Which meant taking her to a hospital might give whoever tried to drop that fucking garage on her another chance to take her out.

A female EMT edged closer. "May I?" she asked softly, motioning to Peyton.

I didn't like it, but until my people could arrive, Peyton needed to undergo at least a cursory exam. And we needed to take care of her shoulder.

Finally, I nodded and carried Peyton over to an ambulance. Her partner, the young guy who'd tried to take her before, wisely stayed a good distance away.

The female EMT was gentle and professional. Her hands were soft and steady as she checked

Peyton's vitals. Then she examined her more thoroughly, wincing when she got to the bruise.

She looked up a moment later. "She's stable. Might have some bruised ribs along with that contusion. No signs of internal bleeding, but she needs a more thorough examination. She's dehydrated and needs fluids."

"I'll get her what she needs."

"She really should be monitored—" the EMT tried again, but I shut her down.

"She will be." I was already reaching for my phone. "But by someone I trust."

I called Blade. "Need a favor."

"You sound like shit. What's wrong?"

"Got called to a collapsed garage. There was a woman inside, and I pulled her out. Minor injuries for the most part, but she's severely dehydrated and needs fluids and a full examination."

"You want me to send a private medic for dehydration?"

"Pretty sure it wasn't an accident," I grunted. "Think it was timed to make sure she was inside when the building blew. I want eyes on her who have the ability to get around hospital protocols and shit. Not gonna give them another shot at her."

Blade's voice sharpened. "Text me your location.

I have a guy not far. He'll bring his rig. Wife's an ER nurse. I'll send her to ride with the woman."

It was the first breath of relief I'd let out since seeing the blast. "Text me when he's close."

There was a pause. Then Blade muttered, "Gonna have to let her go with them, Wrecker."

"Fuck, no," I snarled.

He sighed impatiently. "Planning on bringing her here on the back of your bike, jackass? Think."

The bastard was right, and I fucking hated it. I grunted an agreement and hung up. Then I scooped Peyton off the stretcher and held her close, glaring at anyone who looked like they might approach.

Ten minutes later, a blacked-out ambulance roared up the side street. The doc climbed out—a big guy with a calm presence. His wife came around the back with an IV kit already in hand. She gave me a smile as she approached, and I loosened my grip enough to set Peyton softly onto their stretcher. The nurse slid a needle into Peyton's arm, then patted mine gently.

"You're doing good," she murmured, eyes on my girl. "She's just sleeping now."

"Don't want her waking up without me there."

She smiled kindly, but her eyes held a determined glint. "She needs care that you can't give her at the moment. I promise, I'll make sure she knows who carried her out."

"Don't care if she knows I rescued her," I grunted, my eyes still glued to my girl as they loaded her into the back of the ambulance. "Just want her to know I'm here and won't let anything happen to her."

The woman cocked her head to the side and gave me a half smile. "She's lucky to have you. Honestly, I doubt she'll wake up before we get there."

I nodded once, jaw locked.

They got her situated in the back, and I climbed on my bike, white-knuckled and wired the whole fucking ride.

When we pulled into the compound, the sun had climbed higher. We were having an unusually warm spring, so it baked the small lot between the clubhouse and the clinic. Gravel crunched under my boots as I stalked to the ambulance and opened the back.

"Hand her to me."

The nurse didn't argue, just removed the IV, then nodded. I lifted Peyton against my chest again, one arm around her shoulders—careful not to jostle her injured side much—the other cradling her knees, and carried her straight through the side door of the clinic.

Blade was waiting.

He gestured to an exam room, and I stalked straight into it, turning to face him, keeping Peyton right where she was.

"Gonna have to set her down, Wrecker."

My eyes narrowed with warning, but he just ignored me and pointed at the exam table, one corner of his mouth twitching.

With a frustrated sigh, I got her on a bed, and he went to work. He replaced the first IV the nurse had removed, checked her pupils and wounds, and did a whole lot of other poking and prodding that made me want to rip off his balls. Thank fuck she wasn't awake because if she'd given any indication that she was in pain, Blade's old lady, Elise, wouldn't be havin' any more kids.

"Like the EMT said, she's okay," he finally confirmed. "Little banged up. But nothing serious."

"Good, I'll take her to my room." I moved in to pick her up, but Blade stepped into my path.

"She needs a few more hours of fluids, man. And I still need to monitor for a head injury."

"You said she was fine!" I yelled.

Blade rolled his eyes and started cleaning his

tools. "She is. The cut and swelling on her forehead aren't in a place that usually causes a concussion, but I just want to be sure."

My teeth clenched, but I didn't argue. I knew it wouldn't do me any good.

Blade grinned, shaking his head. "Never thought I'd see the day. Wrecker, losing control over a pair of violet eyes. Didn't have that on my bingo card."

"I haven't lost my fucking control," I snapped.

"Maybe not," he said, voice low, still grinning. "But you're claimed. Just haven't figured out which one of you did the claiming."

I didn't reply.

Just turned back to the bed, grabbed a chair, and dropped onto it.

I watched her breathe.

Listened to the monitor tick.

And told myself I'd never let anything happen to her again.

No matter who I had to tear apart to keep that promise.

4

PEYTON

I woke to the sharp scent of antiseptic and something tugging at my arm. My lashes fluttered open under the glare of bright fluorescent lights, and for a second, I had no idea where I was. The drop ceiling above me didn't provide any clues. All I knew for sure was that my mouth felt dry and my shoulder ached.

Then the fog cleared enough to remember what had happened.

I'd been trapped. Buried.

Panic slammed into my chest like a fist.

I bolted upright, moving too fast for my injuries —whatever they were. Pain flared in my shoulder, sharp and throbbing. I gasped and looked down at my arm, heart hammering as I found an IV line taped to the inside of my elbow.

I reached down with fingers trembling to touch it, but a rough hand closed over mine before I could.

"Don't."

That single word from a deep voice froze me.

My gaze jerked to the source, and my breath caught. A man sat beside the bed, one hand still wrapped gently around mine, his touch steady but firm. His dark brown eyes were vaguely familiar, which made no sense when there was no way I'd ever met him before. This guy was too memorable for me to have forgotten.

"You're okay," he said, softer this time. "You're safe."

My lungs finally expanded as I took him in. The taste of ash lingered on my tongue, and my chest burned. So did my throat, none of which was a surprise considering what I'd just gone through.

Even sitting, I could tell he was tall. And muscular.

His dark hair was messy and had streaks of dust in it, so did the scruff on his cheeks, and his dark jeans, black boots, T-shirt, and leather vest.

I finally realized why his eyes had seemed

familiar—they were the last thing I saw before I passed out.

"It was you."

"I'm the one who found you, yeah." He leaned forward, and I caught a hint of black ink on his chest.

His thumb brushed lightly over the back of my hand, and it sent a shiver down my spine. Not from fear, though. I'd just had a building literally fall on top of me, but I still felt the pull of attraction toward this man. That was how strong it was.

"I..." I glanced around. "Where am I?"

"You're in the clinic at the Iron Rogues compound. You've been out for a few hours, but our club doctor assured me the cut on your head isn't in a spot that would usually lead to a concussion." My brows drew together at his answer, and he lifted his other hand to smooth the line that popped up in my forehead. "Don't worry, baby. Blade will be back to check on you soon. I sent him a text when you started to wake up."

"Good to know, because I think I only caught about half of what you said." I shook my head with a weak laugh. "What's the Iron Rogue compound? Is my doctor really named Blade? And why am I not at the hospital?"

"You seem sharp as a whip to me, so I wouldn't

be too worried." He lowered his arm to tap the front of his leather vest. "I'm part of the Iron Rogues MC. The compound is where our club is based, in Old Bridge. It's the safest place I could bring you for medical attention since Blade has this clinic set up to take care of just about anything that could've been wrong with you. The property is surrounded by a gate that's manned, and a lot of my club brothers are here. Lets me focus on you without havin' to worry about anyone sneakin' up on us."

I sank back against the pillows, more of the tension easing from my body at his explanation. "You pulled me out of the wreckage of that garage and watched over me ever since?"

"Damn fucking straight," he growled. "Wasn't gonna leave you alone when you were vulnerable."

Heat bloomed in my chest, chasing out the last of the fear. No one had ever protected me like that before. Not since my dad had been alive.

The door creaked open, and a man stepped into the room.

"You're awake." He crossed over to us and clapped his hand around my rescuer's shoulder. "Good. I was starting to worry I'd have to stick Wrecker with a sedative if you didn't come around soon."

"Wrecker?" I echoed, glancing at the man still seated beside me.

"Reid." His eyes stayed locked on mine. "Club name's Wrecker. You call me Reid."

The other man, who I assumed was Blade based on the stethoscope around his neck, snorted at Reid's correction, earning himself a quick glare from Reid.

Blade ignored him as he switched to full doctor mode, pressing the cold metal against my back and asking me to take a few deep breaths.

I did and winced halfway through.

"Still sore?"

I nodded.

"Not surprised. You took quite a hit, but nothing's broken. No signs of concussion or internal injury either, which is pretty damn miraculous." He checked the IV. "You're good on fluids now, but you need to drink water and eat hydrating foods. I'm sure Wrecker will make sure that happens."

Reid squeezed my hand. "Yup."

Blade cleared his throat. "Other than that, just rest. Don't push yourself. I'm prescribing some pain medication, but if your shoulder starts to hurt more, your headache gets worse, or anything else seems off, let Wrecker know so I can look you over again."

After pulling the needle from my arm and wrapping it with a bandage and gauze, he murmured, "I'll go grab the meds for you." Then he walked away and closed the door behind him, leaving me alone with Reid again. And so many questions.

Reid didn't move when the door clicked shut behind Blade. He stayed in the chair beside me, his hand still resting over mine like he wasn't ready to let go. Which was lucky for me since I didn't want him to. Not yet.

"Thank you," I whispered. "For pulling me out. Bringing me here. Staying with me. For...all of it."

His jaw ticked. "Don't need your thanks."

"But maybe I need to give it."

His voice was calm, but edged with a gruffness. "Then I'll take it, baby."

I didn't know what to make of him calling me baby like that—or my reaction to hearing it. So I shifted again and blurted, "Can I ask you something?"

He nodded. "Anything."

"How did you get to me so quickly?"

Reid cupped my hand between his palms. "Saw your car where you left it, so I knew you were there. Then a witness said they saw where you entered the structure, so we had a good starting point."

"Crap, my car," I groaned.

"Don't worry, baby," he reassured me. "One of our prospects already went down to Chattanooga to grab it. He'll be back soon."

"But how?" I asked, my eyes widening.

"Think we're looking into the same problem, just not sure what put you on the trail."

I hesitated, mostly out of habit. For months, I'd been playing things close to the vest. Even with my faculty adviser. But after everything Reid had done for me, he'd earned an explanation.

"I want to do my senior capstone project on structural negligence in commercial real estate. To honor my dad since he's the reason I got interested in civil engineering in the first place." My lips curved into a soft smile as I remembered how I'd hoped my dad was watching over me before Reid came to my rescue. "Most of the time, defects get chalked up to lazy contractors or overworked inspectors. I wasn't expecting to find anything different when I started my research, but I found a pattern. A string of building collapses and near misses have occurred over the past five years. There were different names on the deeds, different contractors, and different inspectors. But when I dug deeper, the properties were all connected to the same real estate group, which made me think some kind of corporate fraud was going on."

"Fuck," he bit out, lifting his hand to rake his fingers through his hair.

"Yeah, that was pretty much my reaction too." I heaved a deep sigh. "The parking garage is connected to them. It was only thirty minutes away, so I thought I'd go take a look and see if I could spot anything suspicious. I'm not sure if my infrared camera made it out of the building without any damage, but I also got some good photos on my phone. It's broken, but everything backs up to the cloud, so at least I still have those."

A muscle jumped in his jaw. "Fucking hell, Peyton. You can't put yourself in danger like that. Never again."

"I wasn't expecting the thing to collapse on top of me." This time, I was the one who squeezed his hand. "If the structural issues I found after inspecting the exterior of the garage had been bad enough for that kind of destruction, I never would've gone inside."

Something flared in his dark eyes that made me wonder if he knew more about this morning's catastrophe than I did, but before I could ask, he growled, "It's a damn good thing that I'm gonna keep an eye on you from now on so nothing else can happen to you."

"Only until my car's here and I can go." I wasn't looking forward to leaving anytime soon, but it wasn't as though I could stay here with Reid forever.

"You're not going anywhere."

Her sexy mouth dropped open when I told her she couldn't leave.

The surprise only lasted a moment before her violet eyes narrowed. Then her mouth parted again, like she was ready to argue. But she wasn't able to speak before I leaned closer, and the air between us thickened.

"I'm not trying to play caveman, Peyton," I said, my voice low and rough. Not that I didn't have the desire to be. "But you're not walking out that door without me."

"Because...?" She arched a brow, somehow commanding the room like a queen as if she wasn't half-sitting in a clinic bed with an IV still taped to her hand.

"Because someone wanted you dead, and I'm not fucking letting that happen."

Her breath hitched. It was subtle, but I caught that little spike of fear she tried to hide. And beneath it was confusion. I could tell that a mind like hers didn't like blanks. She wanted to solve the puzzle and hated not knowing what pieces were missing.

I leaned back in my seat and crossed my arms over my chest. "This wasn't a freak accident." Slowly, I walked over and sat in the chair by her bed. "They were waiting for you, baby."

Peyton's lips pressed together, and her throat worked as she swallowed. "You think the building was brought down on purpose."

"I know it was." My gaze dropped to the faint bruising along her collarbone—newer than the ones I'd seen earlier. "The damage pattern didn't match the structural fatigue. It was too clean. Too targeted. But it was expertly masked. I wouldn't have recognized it if I hadn't seen shit like that before."

Her eyes widened. "How?"

I shrugged. "My degree's in civil engineering. Structural integrity, load-bearing analysis, that kind of thing. Got it while I was still active duty." I met her gaze. "Combat Engineer. EOD for Army Special Operations. I know how to bring a building down.

And how to keep one standing when everything else around it crumbles."

She didn't respond, but I saw the curiosity that sparked in her eyes. She wanted to know more, but she wasn't sure if she should ask.

I smiled, thinking about how cute my inquisitive little kitten was, but I was also concerned because, as the saying goes, curiosity killed the cat.

"After I got out, I started contracting," I continued. "Urban Rescue Demolitions. Specialized in collapsed building recovery. Fast entry, tight space clearance, brute-force extractions. Cities or firehouses call me in when shit goes sideways."

Peyton blinked slowly, like she was trying to figure me out but was failing. "So...you're basically the guy they call when there's no path in."

"Exactly." I tilted my head, smiling at her astuteness. "And the second I saw what was left of that garage, I suspected you weren't buried by accident. Then everything I noticed as we worked our way in and out of that building confirmed it."

She swallowed hard, voice barely above a whisper. "I didn't tell anyone I was going there except my roommate. And she would never."

I shook my head and leaned closer, resting my elbows on my bent knees. "Someone else knew." I looked straight into her amazing violet orbs. "And they wanted you gone."

All the color drained from her cheeks. She looked delicate and vulnerable, as if she might break. But there was strength underneath it all, and something told me that if she fell apart, she'd claw her way through anyway. It made me want to wrap her up in my arms and protect her from anything in the world that could bring her pain. But I was also drawn to her courage. She was everything I could ever want and everything I would ever need.

"Why?" she eventually croaked.

I didn't sugarcoat it. "I'm not completely sure yet. But I'm guessing you've been asking too many questions and digging too deep. Kicked a hornet's nest without realizing it."

She blinked, and I saw fear lurking in her violet depths. I hated that she was afraid, and I was even more determined to keep her safe.

"Tell me a little more," I asked, my voice softer. "Why that building?"

Her eyes flicked up to mine, cautious. "There's a pattern. People don't realize it, but by trying to be unpredictable, they usually end up doing the opposite. The timing on this one just fit."

I scratched my chin as I thought over everything

she'd told me. "Most likely, they figured it out when you requested the public information and blueprints. How long ago did you do that?"

She bit her lip as she contemplated my question. "Three days, I think?"

I nodded. "Plenty of time."

"For what?"

"To rig the place so it would blow—with you inside." I stood and began to pace, my energy keyed up over thoughts of what could have happened if I hadn't gotten to Peyton in time. It could have been even worse than before if I had gotten there too late. I wasn't going to let my mind wander down that rabbit hole, so I turned back to the current problem. "Is there anything else you can think of?"

"Well, I'm pretty sure that payouts are happening." She smiled crookedly. "But I don't have the hacking skills to get that information."

Her eyes sparkled as she watched for my reaction to her joke. If she only knew.

I winked at her, and some of the color returned to her cheeks.

Pacing again, I thought about our next steps. "You have proof of what you've discovered so far?"

"I've been compiling it all." Her eyes filled with pride and nerves. "Blueprints. Building specs. Interview notes with locals. Even photos from demo sites. I have everything saved remotely."

I nodded once. "Let me see it."

Her brow furrowed. "I don't even know you."

"You know I carried you out of a collapsed structure that should've killed you." I moved closer to stand directly beside her. "That I brought you to my home, a place very few outsiders are ever invited into. This compound is well hidden to those who don't know the area, baby. We don't take well to outsiders." I leaned down, planting a fist beside each of her hips, caging her in as I bent to put my face inches from hers. "And you know I make your body come alive."

Her blush hit fast and hot.

I pulled back and grinned at her telling reaction. "It's one hundred percent reciprocated, baby," I assured her.

Her blush deepened, and my eyes followed the color down until it disappeared into her shirt. Soon, I was gonna see just how far that sweet pink spread.

Shaking away that thought before I was so hard I couldn't walk, I retreated a little and looked into her deep violet eyes. "And you know in your gut that you can trust me. Just like I knew I could trust you."

She double blinked. "You've only known me for less than a day."

I shrugged. "Long enough."

Peyton stared at me, and I could feel it—her brain fighting her instincts. She wanted logic, evidence. But her intuition was leaning toward me.

After a long moment, she reached for the phone on the rolling tray beside the bed. Her fingers trembled, but her voice was steady. "You can get access through my remote desktop. Password's Renfield3. Open the folder marked Thesis."

I took her cell from her gently and laid it down on the bed. Then I leaned in and clasped her shaky hand between both of mine. "You're safe now, Peyton." My soft tone was backed with steel. "I won't let anything happen to you."

I was tempted to tell her right then that she was mine, but I didn't want to chance her thinking I was crazy and trying to run away.

She exhaled, and all the tension left her body as she melted back against the pillows. Her lashes lowered, and before I could say another word, she was asleep again.

I stood there another moment, just watching her breathe. Then I slipped out and headed for my room.

My laptop sat on the dresser where I'd left it. I

grabbed it and doubled back to the clinic, settling into the battered sofa across from her bed. I retrieved her files, then opened them and began reading.

Blueprints. Permit requests. Notations in the margins. Cross-referenced inspection logs. Safety codes and materials research. There was a mountain of information.

Damn. The girl was good.

As I read through the information, I noticed that several collapses had occurred due to a lack of structural integrity. But something was off about the way the more recent ones came down.

I studied the photos and insurance reports with even more scrutiny until it hit me.

I'd seen this shit before. Staggered fault lines. Reinforced fail points. Structural anchors that were clipped to pull the rest of the load-bearing walls down with them. This wasn't just cutting corners—it was professional demolition. Well disguised, but I was the fucking best in my field. I knew the signs when I saw them.

I fished my phone from my pocket and hit Deviant's contact.

He answered on the first ring. "Wrecker," he greeted gruffly.

"Got a project for you. Tracing shell permits and

false inspection logs. A series of collapsed buildings. The companies and insurance underwriters for each of them are different but all linked to the same real estate company. The last several construction patterns match sabotage I've seen before."

"Send it all," he murmured. "I'm already bored today."

I fired off the docs and notes, then clicked off the call just as Peyton stirred again.

Blade walked in ten minutes later, a clipboard in one hand and a coffee in the other. "She's stable. You can take her outta here but don't let her do anything but sleep, hydrate, and eat."

"I'll set her up in my room."

Blade grinned, one brow raised. "Gonna be able to keep your dick in check for now? She needs actual rest."

I shot him a look. "She's staying with me."

He chuckled and scrawled something on his chart.

"Didn't say she wasn't. Just make sure she rests before you start marking up territory." His smile widened. "Gonna drag her to your room or let her walk?" A growl rumbled in my chest, and he held up a hand. "Hey, just asking. I remember what it's like. Shit moves fast when it's real."

I ignored him and turned to Peyton. She was sitting up slowly, blinking sleep from her eyes.

"Up for a relocation?"

She nodded, face pale but steady. After Blade removed the IV, I helped her swing her legs over the edge of the bed and kept my arm under her back while she stood.

Peyton wobbled a little, so I scooped her up and carried her back to the clubhouse. When we entered the kitchen, Maverick's old lady was sitting at one of the long tables feeding applesauce to their ten-month-old son, Chase.

When Molly looked up and saw us, she laughed. "Didn't take you long."

"Didn't need long," I grunted.

She snorted and went back to her task. "None of you did."

Peyton watched me with curiosity, but I just kept moving through the kitchen and down the hall to my room. After unlocking it, I nudged the door open with my foot and stepped inside.

My bed took up most of the wall on the right side of the room. Beside my desk was a small couch that sat under a window, and the dresser across from it had a bottle of water and a couple of protein bars I'd left there the night before. I gently lowered Peyton onto the mattress and went to my drawers, pulling out a soft black tee.

"You can wear this, baby," I murmured as I tossed it to her. "While you change and get under the covers, I'll get you food."

She nodded again, her eyes wide and mouth parted like she wanted to say something but couldn't find the words.

"Relax," I told her with a wink. I let the door close behind me, rubbing a hand down my face as I stepped into the kitchen. Racer was there, munching on chips while fucking with something on his phone.

He looked up when he heard me, and his lips curved up. "Heard you were moonlighting as Florence fuckin' Nightingale," he joked, after he swallowed. "Your baby bird awake?"

I flipped him off and grabbed a plate and filled it with things that would be easy for Peyton to eat. As I was finishing, I heard Racer chuckle and glared at him.

"Didn't take you for the coddling type. That little girl's got your balls in a chokehold already."

He was saved from my cutting response when my phone buzzed with a new message.

DEVIANT

> Looks like every one of the
> buildings has Eclipse Insurance
> underwriting the projects—they are
> the underwriter for that real estate
> company, too. They used different
> registered corps, but I found the
> link connecting them all to Eclipse.

> Also, a name keeps popping up.

> Ward Calder.

I didn't reply. Just stared at the name until my teeth hurt from how tight I clenched my jaw.

Ward fucking Calder.

He'd been my second when I was in command of my old unit. And a ruthless son of a bitch. Not like me or my club brothers. There had always been something sinister inside him. I'd had to intervene on several occasions when he'd been reckless and almost put our team in jeopardy.

Taking a deep breath, I put his name in the back of my mind. Later. I'd deal with that fucker later.

Tossing Racer one last withering glare, I grabbed the food and went back to my room. Peyton was already tucked in, my shirt nearly swallowing her, her legs pulled up under the blanket.

"Eat," I urged, handing her the plate. "Then sleep."

Her eyes turned soft as she looked over her feast and then she smiled gratefully. "Thank you."

My hand itched to touch her, and I gave in to the impulse, brushing some of her black curls away from her face. I frowned at the dark circles under her eyes, hating the sight of her in any kind of distress.

While she picked at her food, I dragged my laptop to the loveseat and kept one eye on the screen and the other on her.

When she sighed contentedly and told me she was full, I took the plate and set it on my dresser. I turned back to tuck her in and realized she'd already fallen back asleep. Damn, she was gorgeous.

Deviant had sent some information to me, so I went back to work while I watched over her. Fox sent me a couple of updates on club business but didn't ask me to leave Peyton, which I appreciated. He even sent a prospect up with dinner, though Peyton continued to sleep the rest of the day.

Later that night, I climbed into bed beside her, the heat of her body dragging something primal and vicious out of me. I wanted to roll over, pull her beneath me, and fuck her until neither of us remembered our own names. Until she was well and truly claimed.

But she needed rest. And I wasn't gonna fuck that up.

I lay still, eyes on the ceiling, every muscle tight. But she eventually shifted in her sleep, turning toward me and snuggling up close to my body. Her hand landed on my chest, and my fingers circled her wrist. My other arm was around her waist, holding her to me.

I finally relaxed. She was with me. Safe. Warm. Protected.

And mine.

Even if she didn't know it yet.

6

PEYTON

I blinked awake, acutely aware of the weight pressed against my back. I'd never slept with a man before, but I didn't freak out because it could only be one person—Reid.

His warmth surrounded me, his woodsy scent filling my nostrils and providing me with a comfort I hadn't expected. Which was probably why I slept so long.

After taking a nap yesterday morning and then passing out after lunch and sleeping through the night, I figured I'd be up before the sun. Yet somehow, I still felt groggy and heavy-limbed. After being knocked unconscious, it was as though my body decided now was the perfect time to rest in a way I hadn't in too long.

I had a feeling it wasn't just the exhaustion catching up with me. That it was because of Reid, too. Maybe being close to him was enough to flip a switch in my brain and let me shut down safely for a while.

Shifting slightly, I tried not to wake him and felt a tug in my shoulder. It was sore and tight, but not as bad as I expected. The pain was manageable—probably in large part because Reid woke me up in the middle of the night to take pain meds and drink more water.

I let my eyes adjust, a small smile tugging at my lips as I scanned the room. The room was exactly what I'd expect for a guy like Reid—spartan but solid. And incredibly masculine...much like the man himself.

It was a good thing I'd been so tired when he brought me in here yesterday, because there wasn't much furniture besides the bed—just a desk and chair, a small sofa, a bedside table, and a dresser. The lack of clutter left me with only the flat-screen television on the wall for distraction.

And Reid, while he was with me.

I rolled just enough to look over my shoulder, wincing at the sharp pain that lanced through it. Reid was on his side, one arm bent behind his head, the other resting loosely over my waist. The covers had slipped down to his hips, leaving his broad chest bare.

My eyes widened as I took in the black ink on his tanned skin. I'd gotten a small hint of his tattoos yesterday, but now they were fully on display for me.

I was fascinated by the designs inked on his shoulders and pecs, but it was the lettering running down his right side that practically begged my fingers to trace it. Blocky and unfamiliar, the characters went from beneath his ribs all the way down into the waistband of his sweats.

I had no idea what it said, but to my surprise, I had the urge to run my tongue over each letter.

Squeezing my eyes shut for a second, I wondered what the heck was wrong with me. Reid had literally pulled me from a collapsed building yesterday and probably hadn't slept more than a few hours since... and here I was, fantasizing about licking my way down to his happy trail.

I swallowed hard and buried the urge deep. This was my first time feeling this kind of magnetic pull toward a guy, but the timing couldn't be worse.

While I was peeking at his face again, his lashes flickered, then lifted. His dark eyes were instantly alert and locked straight onto mine as though he'd known I was watching him. My breath hitched at the intensity in his gaze, the low rumble of his voice breaking through the quiet. "Morning, baby."

I liked it when he used the endearment yesterday, but my reaction paled in comparison to hearing it from him first thing in the morning when his deep voice was still raspy. I felt the impact of that word in places I probably shouldn't, especially considering I was recovering from nearly being buried alive. But that didn't stop the butterflies from swirling in my belly.

"Morning," I murmured back, suddenly shy despite the fact that we'd just spent the night curled up together.

His mouth curved slightly, as though he knew exactly what kind of thoughts were racing through my mind. "How're you feelin'?"

"Honestly?" I shifted closer to him and took stock of my body again. "Surprisingly good. I mean, my shoulder's still sore as heck, but nothing like yesterday. And my head's relatively clear now that I'm fully awake, which is a nice surprise."

"Glad to hear it." He stretched, the motion making every muscle in his chest ripple as he propped himself up on one elbow. "You must've needed the rest. You were out cold when I came back last night. Didn't even twitch when I climbed into bed."

Heat crawled up my neck and into my cheeks. "You, um...slept next to me?"

That half smile turned into something closer to a smirk, though it still held softness. "Hoped you'd sleep better if I was close. Guess I was right."

He definitely was. I'd never felt more at ease in a strange place, which should've been impossible given everything I'd been through. But being near Reid had anchored me in a way nothing else had. Even sound asleep.

I didn't know what to make of that since we just met each other yesterday.

"I did," I admitted, my voice barely above a whisper. "Thank you."

He didn't say anything right away, holding my gaze as he let the silence stretch. It wasn't awkward, just weighted with something that made my breath catch.

Reid tilted his head toward the door. "You hungry for something heartier than that light shit Blade had you stick with yesterday?"

I thought about it for a moment before shaking my head. "Actually, I think I'd rather shower first, if that's okay. I figure hot water will help with the soreness."

His jaw flexed, the muscles ticking as his nostrils flared. "Of course. I'll get you some ibuprofen, too."

He stood in one fluid motion, my eyes trailing over every inch as his tall frame unfolded. Gray sweatpants hung low on his hips, and his butt looked great in them. After he grabbed a similar pair in black and a matching T-shirt, he strode toward my side of the bed, and I realized the front view was even better.

I finally understood why there were so many memes about guys in gray sweats. And the need for a cold shower...because it was very hot in here all of a sudden.

It took me a second to shake myself out of my stupor when he held a clean T-shirt out to me. "This should work for today."

I briefly considered letting him know that I had a change of clothes in the trunk of my car for when I got dirty in the field, but I preferred the idea of wearing his clothes instead. "Thanks."

Our fingers brushed when I reached out, and a jolt passed between us.

We looked at each other. And for a second, it felt

as though the world had narrowed to just that single point of contact.

Reid was the one to break it. Clearing his throat again, he took a step back, and his hand fell away.

"There are towels, soap, whatever you need in the bathroom."

I nodded, clutching the soft cotton clothes to my chest. "Thanks."

Every line of his body was taut with tension as he turned away. I stepped into the bathroom and shut the door behind me with a firm click.

After turning on the shower so the water could heat, I caught my reflection in the mirror as I peeled off the borrowed T-shirt I slept in.

My shoulder was bruised and still a little swollen. I was only a little tender in a few other places. But still alive.

Because of Reid.

I took a deep breath and stepped into the shower, wincing a little as the spray hit my shoulder. The water was already warm, and steam curled around me until the world outside faded away. I leaned forward, pressing my forehead to the cool tile, and let the heat soak into my skin.

Maybe it was the shock of everything that

happened yesterday finally wearing off. Or the silence.

But all I could think about was Reid.

I squeezed my eyes shut, water streaming down my face. I was trying so hard not to read too much into things and get ahead of myself. But when a man looked at you as though he'd burn the world to keep you safe, it was hard to stay grounded.

I'd hoped the shower would help me get my head on straight, but using his toiletries only made it worse. Now I smelled like him.

After I dried off, I put Reid's clothes on and felt even more surrounded by him.

My breath shuddered as I dragged it into my lungs, my pulse racing.

This wasn't just gratitude. And I didn't think it was only due to hormones either, though those were definitely in play.

My reaction to him was too strong. He'd pulled me from the rubble, but now I was in way over my head in a different way...and I didn't want to climb out.

WRECKER

Steam curled from the bathroom door when it creaked open, drifting in lazy ribbons through the cooler air of my room. I looked up from where I was seated at the end of the bed, boots planted wide, arms braced on my thighs.

Peyton stepped out barefoot, and I froze.

Her hair was damp against her shoulders, and my shirt hung from her frame like a fucking gift-wrapped fantasy. The fabric swallowed her, the hem brushing the tops of her thighs, the sleeves too long, and the collar slouching off one delicate shoulder to reveal her smooth skin and a teasing strip of collarbone. She looked fresh, and her skin was flushed from the heat. Or maybe she'd been thinking about me. Either way, my cock noticed before my brain had a chance to issue a warning.

"You trying to kill me, baby?" I rasped, voice wrecked from the sheer force of holding back.

Her cheeks went pink as her gaze flicked to mine, then away. She fidgeted with the hem of the tee, twisting the material between her fingers. "This was the only thing you gave me to wear."

"Did that for a reason. I like seeing you in my clothes."

The blush deepened, and she bit her lip, her violet eyes flickering with heat. That was all it took. My control frayed like a cut wire.

I was on my feet and across the room before she could suck in another breath. She backed into the wall, eyes widening as I loomed over her. I planted my palms on either side of her head, trapping her there without touching her. My gaze dropped, and I watched her chest rise and fall, fast and shallow. When I looked up at her eyes again, her pupils were blown wide. Those bright violet eyes were locked on me with something between awe and anticipation.

"You look so fucking sweet like this," I muttered, dipping my head. "So fucking innocent."

She shivered, and I felt the tremor all the way to

my bones. Unable to hold back anymore, my mouth slammed down on hers.

The kiss started hard, hungry and desperate. My mind shouted for me to be gentle, but lust coursed through my body, my blood roaring in my ears and drowning out the voice of reason.

Then she melted into me, her hands clutching the front of my shirt, her mouth opening on a soft, needy whimper. I took full advantage. Plunging my tongue deep, I claimed every inch of her mouth. She tasted like desire, along with cinnamon and some-thing unique to only her. It was fucking addictive.

When her knee brushed my thigh, I grabbed her hips. "Put your arms around my neck, baby. Don't wanna hurt your shoulder."

When she'd done as I'd instructed, I hoisted her up. She gasped, her legs locking around me as I pressed her tight to the wall. The scent on her skin was mine and drove me half feral.

"You don't get it yet," I growled against her mouth. "But you will. I'm gonna ruin you for anyone else. Make you come so hard you forget your own name."

She moaned, and it sounded like pure sin. My hand slid between us, fingertips finding the hem of the shirt covering her and yanking it up. A low, primal groan rumbled out of me when I realized she wore nothing underneath.

"Fuck, Peyton," I hissed, burying my face in the curve of her throat. Her skin was hot, still damp from the shower, and softer than anything I'd ever touched.

My hands cupped her ass and pressed her closer as I ground my erection against her, hard enough to make her cry out. Then my other hand slipped between us, my fingers dragging through her folds, finding her slick and ready. I teased her sweet pussy until she was panting and trembling, digging her nails into my shoulders like she wanted to claw her way inside me.

Her climax hit fast and sharp, her whole body clenching tight around my fingers. She came with a cry that echoed around the room and vibrated in my chest. I kissed her through her release, groaning against her lips and damn near losing control.

I was seconds away from fucking her right there —wall, bed, floor, didn't matter—when a sharp knock shattered the moment.

I froze, my breath caught halfway in my throat, my eyes locked on Peyton. She was panting, her cheeks flushed, hair mussed, shirt askew and clinging to her curves like a fuckin' dream. My hand was still between her thighs, drenched in her juices.

One more minute, and I'd have been buried in her.

Whoever was on the other side of that door was about five seconds from being gutted.

I gritted my teeth and gently lowered Peyton to the floor. Her legs were unsteady, her lips kiss-swollen, and her eyes glazed. Then I stalked over to the door and yanked it open, already scowling.

Deviant stood there, brows raised, holding a brown paper bag that smelled like bacon and cinnamon. "You ignoring your phone on purpose, or just forgot how it works?"

"Busy," I growled.

Deviant snorted. "Sure. Busy being balls-deep or tongue-tied between thighs you're planning to keep."

My eyes narrowed, my frustration growing. "Alice send you because she's lookin' to host a funeral?"

I was about to shut the door in his face when he slapped a hand on the hard surface to keep it open.

"Here for Fox," he muttered. Then held up the bag he was carrying. "But Alice told me to bring you this. She said you were both probably starving. And also that, and I quote, 'If you don't want Wrecker to become a feral bastard, feed him something besides adrenaline and bad decisions.' Like I'm the fuckin' breakfast fairy now."

"Guess you finally found your calling, princess," I grunted, snatching the bag from his hand.

Deviant smirked, completely unfazed. "Keep fuckin' around, Wrecker, and you'll be eating through a straw."

"Get fucked."

"Already did." His amused grin faded to a serious look. "Fox called a meeting. And before you ask—yeah, he means now. Don't make him come drag your ass out."

"Gimme a fucking minute," I snarled.

"Try not to rip anyone's face off on the way down." He tossed the last word over his shoulder as he started down the hall.

"Depends on who's in my fucking way," I grunted, slamming the door shut.

When I turned back around, Peyton was still leaning against the wall, chest heaving and her lashes lowered like she was trying to process what the hell just happened.

I didn't let her see the frustration bleeding out of

me as I walked back to her. After pulling a breakfast sandwich out of the bag, I pressed it into her hands and brushed a kiss over her mouth before carrying her over to the bed. "Eat and rest, baby. I'll be back soon."

She nodded, dazed.

I hated leaving her. But I wasn't about to keep Fox waiting. Still, I left the room with fury simmering just beneath the surface. Wolfing down the food while I headed downstairs didn't dim it much.

When I stalked into my prez's office, he was seated behind his desk, eyes sharp as ever. Maverick leaned against the wall with his arms crossed and an unreadable expression on his face. Most of our other officers and a few enforcers were scattered throughout the room, tension lacing the air.

Hawk, Storm, Midnight, and Nevada were seated at the round conference table.

"'Bout fuckin' time," Whiskey grunted. "Thought maybe you'd gotten swallowed whole."

"Still might," I muttered, dropping into the seat beside him.

Nevada smirked. "So I'm guessin' you forgot how to work your phone cause your face was buried and your brain shot to hell."

"You got a death wish?" I asked, voice low. "Or just bored of breathing?"

Viper barked a laugh. "You wanna keep all your teeth, Nevada, I'd shut the fuck up."

I nodded at him, sprawled on the old couch in the sitting area. Inferno and Racer took up the over-stuffed chairs across from it.

Fox cleared his throat. "Enough. We've got business."

The jokes stopped, just like that. When Fox spoke, everyone listened.

He gave a rundown of a couple of minor club issues—nothing urgent. Then he turned to me. "Deviant filled me in on some of it, but I want to hear everything. Tell me about Peyton."

I laid it all out. The garage, her research, the collapse patterns. I told them about her thesis, how she'd been digging too deep and got herself noticed. The minute I mentioned shoddy materials and the signs of charges, every man in the room sharpened. Like predators scenting blood.

"You think she was targeted?" Fox asked.

"Yeah. She was askin' questions someone didn't want answered. And those buildings? They didn't fall on their own. Some of 'em were rigged. I'd bet my patch on it."

Deviant nodded. "I've started tracing permits and supplier invoices. Already flagged a couple of anomalies."

Fox leaned back, gaze heavy. "Then we hit this from all angles. Legal, digital, boots on the ground. Stone'll handle any legal pressure. Deviant, keep digging. The rest of you—eyes open. If anyone comes sniffing around, I wanna know."

I looked around the room and felt something settle in my chest. Not peace. Not calm. But purpose. These men—my brothers—weren't just lethal. They were loyal. This was blood, just not by birth. We weren't clean, but we had limits, honor, and a code. Our own brand of justice.

In certain circles, it was well-known that we protected those who couldn't protect themselves by any means necessary. And when it called for blood, we made sure justice bled out on the floor.

They'd have my back on this.

When the meeting broke, I jumped to my feet, ready to get back to Peyton, but Hawk grinned like he'd been waiting the whole meeting just to run his mouth. "Runnin' off to take care of your woman?"

I sighed, knowing what was coming. And that I deserved it.

He barked a gruff laugh. "You talked all that shit

when I fell for Gemma. What was it you said? That I was whipped so hard I squeaked when she looked at me?"

I scratched my jaw and let out a grunt. "Yeah. And turns out I was a fuckin' idiot."

A few of the guys laughed, low and rough. Maverick shook his head, a ghost of a smile cutting across his usually unreadable face.

"Hell," Hawk said, his mouth curved smugly. "Didn't think I'd live long enough to hear you admit that."

"Don't get used to it," I growled.

Racer stood and walked over to stand by Fox's desk, shit-eating grin in place. "So we calling it now? Wrecker's officially owned."

The room went still for half a second—just long enough for Fox to cut in, voice calm and cool with steel underneath. "Careful, Racer. One more word like that, and you'll be eating it."

Racer blinked, clearly not expecting that. "I was just joking—"

Storm smirked. "Yeah, and the last guy who joked about mine ended up limping for a week."

Whiskey chuckled, shaking his head as he sipped from a chipped mug. "You keep flappin' your mouth, kid, and you're gonna jinx yourself. Next time we blink, you'll be writing poetry and makin' your woman breakfast in bed."

"I don't—" Racer started, but Maverick cut him off with a slap to the back.

"Oh, you will. Mark my words. You'll be next. And when it hits? It'll drop you to your fuckin' knees."

"Like the rest of us," Whiskey added, deadpan.

I couldn't help chuckling as I headed back to my woman.

Maverick caught me just outside the door. "Want me to get a property vest made?"

"Yeah," I said without hesitation. "She's mine."

Back in my room, the light filtering through the blinds was soft. Peyton was curled in the sheets, her breathing uneven like she was caught between sleep and waking. When she shifted restlessly and whimpered, I kicked off my boots, removed my shirt, and eased onto the bed before pulling her against me. She made a soft sound and tucked her head beneath my chin before settling.

It happened a few more times, so I didn't let myself fall asleep. I wanted to make sure I was alert in case she needed me to soothe her nightmares.

As I stared down at her beautiful face, a wave of possessiveness crashed over me.

I used to think my brothers were all fucking crazy. Thought love made a man weak.

Now I knew better.

It made you a dangerous son of a bitch.

And I'd turn heaven to ash and hell to ice before I let anything hurt her.

My dream started off innocently enough, but it quickly twisted into a nightmare I'd already lived, starting with the heavy silence. The kind that came right before something terrible was about to happen.

I stood inside the parking garage again, light filtering through cracks in the ceiling, casting long shadows across the floor. My fingers clutched my infrared camera, and everything felt wrong. The air was too still.

Then the rumble started.

A deep, shuddering groan that vibrated up from the concrete. I turned, heart pounding, and saw the ceiling begin to sag. Dust rained from above. Metal creaked. My body wouldn't move fast enough.

The collapse came too quickly. I couldn't make it to the stairwell. There was nothing to protect me from the wreckage.

My scream ripped from my throat as I stumbled, falling backward. The walls closed in.

Something crashed near my head. I couldn't breathe. I couldn't—

I jerked awake with a gasp, my lungs tight and chest heaving.

I wasn't trapped. And I wasn't alone.

A strong arm banded around my waist, grounding me. A low murmur brushed against the back of my neck, the deep voice unmistakable. "Easy, baby. You're safe."

Reid had rescued me from my bad dream, just like he had from that parking garage.

The tension in my body drained at the sound of his voice, my heart still racing but slowing as the nightmare receded. His warmth surrounded me, his powerful body curled protectively around mine like a living shield.

"It was the garage." I swallowed the lump in my throat. "I was back there, but I couldn't get to safety."

"It was just a bad dream, baby." His lips brushed the shell of my ear. "You're safe now. I have you."

I turned so I could see his face in the shadows. "How did you know?"

"You were restless. Figured I'd hold you in case the dreams got bad."

"They did," I whispered. "The last thing I wanted was to relive that whole thing. I'm so glad you pulled me out of it."

His gaze flicked between my eyes. "You trust me, baby?"

I didn't hesitate. "Yes."

Something raw and real shifted in his expression.

"I won't let anything happen to you. Not again."

I believed him. He hadn't given me any reason not to.

Without another word, I nestled closer, letting the steady rhythm of his breathing calm me. Somehow, wrapped in his arms, the fear couldn't touch me.

I wasn't sure how long we lay there in silence, his body warm and secure at my back, his breath brushing softly against my skin. Eventually, I turned to face him again, needing to see him in this quiet moment.

My gaze drifted lower, lingering on the tattoos inked across his chest and shoulders. "Can I ask about the one on your ribs?"

A flicker of pain passed through his dark eyes before he nodded. "Wanted to do something to honor the guys from my team who didn't make it home from overseas."

He'd told me some about his background, so it wasn't hard to guess that he was talking about his military days. "You don't have to tell me more."

He held my gaze, the air between us heavy. "Felt like we were all young and dumb back then, even when I was doing EOD for Spec Ops."

His low voice was haunted. I reached for him without thinking, pressing my palm lightly against the inked skin just over his ribs. I didn't ask what it said. Somehow, I knew the words weren't meant to be shared—just carried.

"I'm sorry," I whispered.

He wrapped his hand around my wrist to hold my palm in place. "I carry them with me every day, but the weight is lighter with you by my side."

His confession touched me so deeply, and I wanted to share another piece of myself too.

"My dad died when I was sixteen. It was a construction site accident. Faulty beams because someone cut corners where it counted most. That's what started me down this path. I didn't want to be another person looking the other way."

His thumb brushed against my cheek. "He'd be proud of you." I smiled faintly, but before I could reply, he added softly, "I am."

My breath caught in my throat. "You don't even know me."

"I'm startin' to."

I didn't pull away. Couldn't, even if I wanted to.

His hand stayed cupped around my cheek, anchoring me to him. We stared into each other's eyes for a long moment, something quiet and solid blooming in the space between us.

A knock sounded at the door, interrupting the moment. Reid's jaw clenched as he rolled onto his back, a low growl rumbling in his throat.

"Fuckin' timing," he muttered, scrubbing a hand over his face before raising his voice. "Yeah?"

"Need to check in on Peyton," came the muffled reply.

I sat up, tugging the covers a little higher, even though I was wearing an oversized shirt. "It's okay."

The tension in Reid's shoulders eased when he heard Blade's voice. He rolled off the mattress, grabbing a tee off the chair and yanking it over his head. Then he strode across the room and jerked the door open. "Hey."

Blade stepped inside. "Sorry it's so early. I'm on

my way to the hospital but wanted to make sure Peyton was still good before I started my shift."

"Thanks, man." Reid clapped him on the shoulder. "Appreciate it."

I flashed a smile at Blade. "Yes, thank you."

Reid crossed his arms and leaned against the wall while Blade turned to me. "Mind if I take a look?"

I shifted, making room for him to sit on the edge of the mattress. "My shoulder's still sore, but not nearly as bad as yesterday. I haven't needed the prescription pain meds."

"Good," Blade said, carefully examining the bruising. "No signs of deeper damage, which means you should heal up nicely. You'll probably be achy for a few more days. Keep up with the ibuprofen, hydrate, and try not to overdo it."

"I'll make sure of it," Reid cut in.

Blade didn't even blink. "Of course you will."

His dry tone made me bite back a smile.

Blade reminded me of warning signs to watch for, then he stood. "You're doing well. I'll check in again tomorrow."

"Thanks," I said, genuinely grateful.

As Blade passed Reid on his way out, he muttered under his breath, "Keep takin' good care of her."

Reid dropped his arms to his sides. "Don't need you to remind me."

The door shut behind Blade with a solid click.

We just got settled back in bed when Reid's phone buzzed from the nightstand, vibrating hard enough to rattle against the wood. He glanced at the screen, his expression darkening as he picked it up.

Turning slightly away from me, he muttered, "What do you need, Deviant?"

His tone was all business—low, rough, and clipped.

I couldn't hear what Deviant said, but I watched Reid's shoulders tense. His hand flexed around his phone.

"Send it to me," he said after a moment. "We'll take a look."

He ended the call and stared at the screen for a beat. "Deviant found security footage from a couple of different sites."

My stomach tightened. "What kind?"

His jaw clenched. "Of someone tampering with the foundation supports. No doubt it was intentional damage. More fucking sabotage."

I sat up straighter, adrenaline kicking in fast. "How many sites?"

"More than one. That's all he said so far."

There was a beat of silence before Reid grabbed the laptop off his desk and opened his email. Tapping on the first video, he sat down next to me so we could both watch. The quality wasn't great— grainy nighttime footage from a motion-activated camera. A man moved through the shadows, crouching near one of the load-bearing beams. His face never turned fully toward the camera.

"Something is familiar about his profile," Reid muttered, sounding frustrated.

We watched another clip. Different site, same figure. Same gait—moving with purpose, knowing exactly where to go and what to do.

"Do you recognize him?" I asked.

Reid exhaled slowly, shaking his head. "Feels like I should. Can't place from where, though. The connection is right fucking there, but I can't quite grab it."

He shook his head, then watched me for a long second, then settled the computer on my lap. "There's more. Deviant sent over everything he's got —video, permits, site maps. We want you to go through it all."

My eyes widened. "Me?"

"You're the one who's been studyin' this shit," he

explained gruffly. "You have the instincts, and you already found patterns everyone else missed."

I felt the weight of what he was asking but not in a bad way. It was heavy but also meant he trusted me. That I wasn't just some girl who'd been in the wrong place at the wrong time. I was part of this now.

I nodded. "Okay. Let's figure this out."

I'd been reviewing the files for at least an hour, combing through site maps and inspection reports Deviant had dug up when a familiar name stopped me cold.

Little Horizons Children's Library.

I clicked into the linked file with growing dread. It was a small, nonprofit renovation project to retrofit an old firehouse into a neighborhood library. It had been part of the same construction initiative I'd flagged in my thesis research after the back portion of the building collapsed a week after the final walk-through.

I opened the corresponding footage.

The man we still couldn't identify crouched beside the rear foundation wall, moving with the same quiet precision we'd seen before. A few minutes later, he vanished into the shadows.

Nobody had been in that building when it fell, but there could easily have been kids there.

My breath hitched. "Reid."

He looked up immediately from the screen of his cell. One glance at my face, and he was beside me in two long strides. "What is it?"

I pointed at the screen, barely able to speak through the tightness in my throat. "The Little Horizons Children's Library collapse? It wasn't an accident. That building was sabotaged. On purpose. And the guy who did it—he's the same one from the other sites."

Reid scanned the screen, jaw clenching. I could see the fury boiling behind his eyes.

"We have to go to the police with this," I whispered, my voice trembling.

His expression hardened in an instant. "No."

"Why?"

"The club will handle it."

I slammed the laptop shut and stood. "Children could have been killed, Reid."

His expression was set in stone. "The system fails people like them all the damn time. Like your dad. That bastard in the video isn't gonna walk free because some asshole with a badge decides he's too rich or too useful to prosecute."

I understood as well as anyone where he was coming from, but that didn't mean I wasn't going to question this call. "You can't just decide you're above the law."

"No," he growled, "but I can damn well make sure justice gets served when the law turns a blind eye. Those buildings never would've collapsed in the first place if these bastards weren't paying people off."

My hands curled into fists at my sides. "They need to be held accountable."

Reid took a step closer, his body radiating fury and control in equal measure.

"You want justice?" he snarled. "Then let me handle this, baby. When we're done, there won't be a single brick left of their empire."

Maybe I should've pushed back harder. Or walked away, demanding space, something to clear my head. Because everything about what Reid had just said terrified me...but not for the reasons it should've.

I wasn't scared of Reid. Only what I was starting to feel when he looked at me like that. When his voice dropped low and dangerous, every cell in my body reacted to his intensity.

Reid's chest rose and fell with uneven breaths,

his gaze locked on mine. I felt that raw, electric thread neither of us had been willing to name yet snap between us.

I didn't look away. Didn't run. I couldn't.

The tension between us sizzled. I was practically vibrating from the strain of holding myself back.

Peyton was clearly feeling it too because her deep purple orbs were dark and bright with heat. Then she took me by surprise when a tenacious glint entered them, and she crossed her arms. Her mouth was set in that stubborn line I was learning meant she was about to drive me outta my fucking mind.

"Fine," she huffed. "If you and the club are going to handle it, then I want in."

I raised a brow, already knowing where this was going—and not liking it one fucking bit. "What the hell does that mean?"

She straightened her spine, chin lifted and violet

eyes flashing. "I can go to the sites. If I'm there in person, maybe I'll notice something the videos didn't catch. I know what to look for."

"No." My voice came out low and sharp.

"Reid—"

I stepped closer, looming over her smaller frame. "No fucking way. You're not setting foot near one of those buildings. Not while someone out there wants to shut you up."

"I'm not made of glass, Reid." Her voice shook, not with fear but fire. "You can't just wrap me in bubble wrap because you think I'm gonna break."

"The hell I can't." My tone turned rougher, harsher, because I could already see it. Her boots on concrete. A crack in the floor. Dust floating in the air like it had that day I found her. And her body buried under steel and debris while I clawed through hell to get to her.

Her mouth parted, and she blinked, like she hadn't expected that level of fury from me. "You said you trusted me to help."

"I do." I raked a hand through my hair, jaw tight. "But there's a difference between helping and painting a fucking target on your back."

"You're a target now, too," she snapped, eyes

burning. "You think they don't know we're working together? I can't stay here in a locked room forever!"

I breathed through my nose, chest heaving. She wasn't wrong, but it didn't matter because reason didn't live in my body when it came to her.

Only instinct.

Only need.

Only the gut-deep drive to *keep her*—safe, whole, fucking mine.

"You don't get it," I ground out. "I *can't* let anything happen to you."

Her eyes softened, but her voice stayed strong. "Then stop treating me like I'm weak. I've survived shit too, Reid. Maybe not combat, but loss, grief, and fear. I can do hard things."

"You don't know what I'll do if I lose you," I snapped. "You still don't get it. So let me make it real fucking clear. I haven't stopped looking at you since I saw your picture, Peyton. You're not just some case to me. I protect what's mine. And I'm telling you right now—you're mine."

The air between us crackled, and the silence that fell wasn't calm. It was volatile. That tight, stretched wire between us finally pulled too taut.

Then it snapped.

Before my mind could catch up, my body was moving, and in one stride, I was on her.

My hands gripped her hips as I slammed my mouth down on hers, kissing her hard, almost enough to bruise. She gasped into me, lips parting, and I took what I wanted—biting, tasting, claiming. Her body arched into mine as she clutched my shoulders like she needed something to hold on to.

All that sass and defiance had turned my cock to stone, but when she melted against me in a rush of heat, I was filled with the primal desire to own her. To mark her. To make her mine in every way.

Peyton had no fucking clue the kind of beast she'd just unleashed.

I spun her around, crowding her backward until her knees hit the bed. Then I shoved the laptop aside and gently pressed her onto the mattress, being mindful of her shoulder as I braced myself above her. The shirt she wore—mine—was wrinkled and clinging to her curves. *Fucking hell, she was gorgeous.*

Her breath came in short pants. Her cheeks were flushed, lips kiss-swollen, and her eyes...they were shimmering, pupils blown so wide they swallowed the violet.

"You wanna know how rough I can be without

breakin' you, baby?" I growled, my voice pure gravel as I dragged the hem of the shirt up her thighs.

Her breath caught. "Y-yes."

I stilled. My gaze snapped to hers. "Yeah?"

She bobbed her chin in a slight nod, her tongue darting out to wet her lips. "I want you, Reid. I want this. I'm not scared of you."

Fuck. That undid me like nothing else could.

"I'll never hurt you," I rasped, my hand cradling her cheek. "But I will fuck you like I own every inch of you. Because I do." My touch was gentle, but my tone was firm. "You know it, don't you?"

She nodded again, voice breathless. "Yes."

I pressed my forehead to hers. "Tell me you're mine."

Her eyes softened, and she whispered, "I'm yours."

My control fucking shattered.

I gripped the front of the shirt and ripped it open with one brutal tug, the fabric tearing down the middle. Peyton gasped, her chest rising and nipples pebbled from the cool air.

"You're gonna kill me, baby," I muttered, dragging my thumb over one perfect peak. "But fuck if I won't die happy."

She blushed so hard that I felt the heat of it radiating from her body. My cock was practically weeping—her innocence was every bit as much of a turn on as her sass.

"Fuckin' perfect," I growled, bending to suck one tight bud into my mouth. Her back arched off the bed, a cry breaking from her throat.

I moved lower, trailing kisses down the soft swell of her stomach. When I reached the gentle slope to her center, I kissed it almost reverently. But the mouthwatering scent quickly filled me with raw, intense hunger.

My hands gripped her thighs and pulled them wide, baring that pretty little pussy to me.

"Damn, baby," I breathed. Her skin was flushed everywhere, all the way down to the insides of her thighs, where she was pink, swollen, and so already wet and shiny for me.

"You're fuckin' soaked, baby." My voice came out gritty, rough with need. "Your pussy aching? Throbbing and empty?"

Peyton licked her lips and nodded.

"Want me to make it better?" I lightly brushed her clit with my thumb.

"Yes," she gasped.

"Not good enough," I rasped, teasing her with my breath as I hovered right above her slick folds. I blew gently over her clit, and she shuddered, making me grin devilishly. "Beg me, baby."

She let out a shaky breath. "Please."

"You can do better than that, Peyton."

Her eyes narrowed, some of that fire returning and causing come to leak from my cock.

I licked her little bundle of nerves, then blew on it again. Her back arched, and her pussy gushed with desire.

"Reid," she moaned. "Please. Oh, please touch me."

Hearing her say my name as she begged me to eat her pussy was like lighting a match that exploded into a furious fire.

I dragged my tongue through her juices and groaned like a starving man getting his first sip of water. She tasted like heaven—sweet and soft and mine. Her legs shook as I licked her again, and she cried out. I focused on her tight little clit, teasing circles until she writhed beneath me, keeping her on edge until she was primed. Then I pinched the bud and plunged my tongue inside her.

She came with a choked cry, her hands fisting the sheets, and her hips bucking as I lapped up every drop she gave me. Only then did I crawl up her body, settling between her thighs, my cock hard and straining against my jeans.

"You ever been with anyone before, baby?" I asked, though I was confident I already knew the answer.

She shook her head, cheeks flushing. "No."

Mine.

The word burned through me, leaving a wake of powerful flames that ate at my control until it was nothing but ash.

I kissed her again as I reached down and popped the button on my jeans, pushing them down far enough to free my cock. When I pressed the tip against her entrance, I looked into her eyes.

"Last chance to tell me to stop," I growled. I didn't know how the fuck I'd do it, but if she needed more time, I would give it to her.

"I don't want you to stop," she said, voice shaking but sure.

"Fuck, yeah," I sighed, sending my thanks to the universe.

I pushed inside, just the head at first, gritting my teeth as her tight heat welcomed me. Damn, she was snug—scorching hot and velvet-soft, wrapping around me like she was made for me. Only me.

Knowing I would be the only cock to ever be inside her...it had the beast clawing to be free.

Her body suddenly tensed beneath mine, and I stilled my hips as I brushed my thumb over her cheek. "You okay?"

She nodded, blinking up at me nervously. "Just... um. You're big."

"Yeah, baby. I am." I smirked, even as sweat beaded on my skin from holding back. "Gonna pop your cherry and fill you with all ten inches of my thick cock. I'm gonna stretch you open until you take every fucking inch." I took her lips in a deep kiss, then dropped my head so my mouth was at her ear. "But it won't break you, baby. Because this virgin pussy was made for me. And only me."

Peyton's breath hitched, and her pupils turned dark and wild. "I want it. Take me, Reid."

I groaned, pushing deeper, inch by inch, until I reached her barrier. Though I would normally hate the idea of causing her any pain, knowing I was about to make her irrevocably mine...drove me fucking wild. I would mark her. Claim her. Fucking own her.

My hips punched forward, driving my dick into her sheath until I was fully seated. "Mine!" I yelled.

Her breath came out in a sharp gasp, her thighs

trembling around me. So I held still, letting her adjust, pressing kisses to her mouth, her jaw, the hollow of her throat. Eventually, her body relaxed, and I started to move.

Slow thrusts at first. Deep. Deliberate. Driving us both to madness.

Peyton's nails bit into my back, and her hips rolled up to meet mine. Every time I hit her cervix, then dragged along her walls as I pulled out, a ragged moan fell from her lips.

"So fuckin' tight," I gritted out, the words rough as gravel. "Made just for me. This pussy was built to take my cock, baby."

"I was," she whispered, voice wrecked, breath catching on every thrust.

My rhythm turned rougher, almost brutal, as I sank deeper with every stroke. The room filled with sounds of skin slapping, her breathy moans, my rough growls, and the slick slide of me claiming her over and over again.

"Fuck, yeah," I grunted, one hand gripping her hip hard enough to bruise. "That's it. Take it. Take all of me, baby. Fucking squeeze me. Squeeze that cock like you're tryin' to milk me dry. Oh fuck, yes!"

"Yes, yes, yes," she chanted, voice climbing,

thighs trembling around me as her sweet little pussy throbbed and fluttered around my shaft. "Oh yes, Reid!"

"Yeah, you feel me, baby?" I rasped, slamming into her so hard the bed creaked under us. "Feel what I'm doin' to you? Gonna fuckin' ruin you from the inside out."

"Yes, Reid. *Please*, I—"

My cock spurted some jizz, and the thought of it taking root sent me into a fucking frenzy. But I stilled and grabbed her chin, forcing her to look straight into my eyes.

"Are you on birth control?"

It took a second for my question to sink in, then her eyes went wide with shock, and I had my answer. I wanted to beat on my chest like a damn caveman as I resumed pounding her into the sheets.

"Gonna fill you up," I growled, cutting her off as her eyes rolled back. "Breed this tight little pussy just like it's meant to be. You want that, don't you? You want me to fuck my come so deep it takes?" Her walls clamped down even harder. "Oh fuck! Your body knows it. It's fucking sucking me in, fighting to let me go."

She sobbed, nodding frantically, lips parted in a

desperate moan. "Yes! I want it. I want all of you. Please!"

I fucked her through the screams that ripped from her throat when her orgasm slammed into her, her pussy clenching so hard around me it stole the breath from my lungs. She was pure heat and silk, writhing beneath me, made to take every thick inch I gave her.

The second I felt her clamp down around me, my own release hit. I roared her name as I spilled inside her, driving deep and grinding my hips against hers. I didn't stop until I'd filled her to the brim.

But I wasn't done. Not even close.

I pulled out and quickly discarded my jeans before I flipped her over, keeping an arm around her waist to make sure there was no pressure on her shoulder, then dragged her hips up beneath me so her back arched and that sweet, swollen pussy was open and glistening. I drove my hard dick back into her heat until she stretched around the base of my cock.

My thick cream dripped down her shaking thighs, and her body trembled like she'd already been wrung out. But when I urged her up onto her knees, so her back was against my chest, she turned her head to look back at me. There was heat burning in her eyes—hazed, glassy, and dazed—but needing more.

And I was gonna give it to her.

"Not enough," I growled, pushing back in so deep she cried out. "You want me to breed you, baby? Then you fucking come again. While I'm filling this pussy up or it's not gonna take."

"Reid...I can't. It's too much," she whimpered, before biting her bottom lip hard, fingers clutching at the sheets.

"You can, baby," I gritted, my jaw clenched. "You fucking will."

I reached around her and between her thighs, rubbing her rigid clit in small, relentless circles while I thrust so deep I hit her cervix and ground into her with every snap of my hips. My other hand stayed locked on her waist, holding her in place, owning every inch of her. She was so small compared to me, so fucking perfect and made for me to hold and fuck her full.

"That's it," I urged, my voice dark and rough. "Let go for me, baby." Her breath caught again, her thighs trembling even harder. "Milk my cock. Gonna come so deep it leaks out for days. Gonna fuck a baby into you so you never forget who you belong to."

"Reid—" Her voice cracked on my name, then turned into a long, drawn-out cry. Her pussy clenched around me so hard it dragged my climax out of me like a fucking trigger pull.

"Fuck! Oh fuck, yes!" I shouted, hips jerking. "Suck me dry, baby. Fuckin' take all of it!"

I came hard, deep, and savage—pouring into her with a raw groan, pushing until I was sheathed to the hilt as I pumped her full of my come. My eyes rolled back, my forehead was damp with sweat, and my chest heaved as I stayed buried inside her, making sure not a single drop went to waste.

When I was finally empty, I stayed fully embedded in her heat as I gently lowered her to the bed, making sure I didn't put any weight on her injury. Then I leaned forward and kissed the space between her shoulder blades. She was still pulsing around me, her body shaking with the aftershocks, breaths ragged and uneven.

"Never letting you go, Peyton," I rasped against her skin, still thick and deep inside her, despite coming twice. "You were made to belong to me."

She turned her head just enough for me to catch the dazed, blissed-out look on her flushed face. Her lashes fluttered, and her lips parted like she wanted to say something, but no words came.

There wouldn't be any.

Because deep down, she already knew it was true.

10

PEYTON

I woke to a faint stream of light peeking through the blinds. The sheets were warm, but when I reached out, the space beside me was cold and empty.

Reid was gone.

My pulse sped up for a second until I spotted the black leather cut folded neatly at the foot of the bed. A small square of paper rested on top of it.

I sat up slowly, wincing at the ache in muscles I didn't know I had, and soreness between my legs. Tugging the blanket with me, I reached for the note.

Had to take care of club business. Don't leave the room unless you're wearing this.

- R

The bold scrawl was unmistakably his. I traced over the letters with a soft smile.

The message wasn't long or flowery, but it didn't have to be. His care for me came through loud and clear.

Warmth bloomed in my chest, twisting up with something fluttery and completely ridiculous. I lost my virginity to a broody biker with protectiveness in his touch, and now he wanted me to wear his cut when I was around his club brothers. The women in the clubhouse wore property patches. That was what Reid had called them when I asked. This wasn't quite the same, but that didn't lessen the impact of him giving it to me.

After taking a shower to ease my aches—the ones from Reid popping my cherry more noticeable than my shoulder—I smiled as I pulled on a pair of leggings and a loose top from the pile of clothes Reid had someone get for me yesterday. Then I picked up the cut and lifted it to my face, breathing in his woodsy scent. I liked knowing I'd be surrounded by it all day.

The vest hung heavy on my shoulders as I shrugged it on, nearly swallowing my frame, the bottom hem brushing the tops of my thighs. I walked into the bathroom, and when I caught my reflection in the mirror, something about the sight made me stand up straighter.

Even when he wasn't here, Reid was still looking out for me. Trusting me with the symbol of the brotherhood that meant so much to him. That knowledge gave me the confidence I needed to explore the clubhouse without him.

I cracked the door open and peeked out. Padding into the hallway with only socks on my feet, I wandered downstairs.

With my stomach growling, I headed straight for the kitchen. I barely made it three steps inside before a curvy brunette spotted me.

"Look what the cat dragged in." She set down her coffee mug with a clink. "You must be Peyton."

I nodded, offering a sheepish smile. "Guilty."

"I'm Gemma, Hawk's old lady. And that's Alice." She gestured toward a redhead seated at the table with twin toddlers on either side. "Greg and Gus belong to her and Deviant."

"Your husband is the computer guy." I beamed a smile at Alice but kept the details slim since I wasn't sure how much the guys shared with their women.

"Yup, he has magic fingers." Gemma and I giggled, making Alice blush. "When he's at his keyboard. Geesh, get your minds out of the gutter."

Gemma handed me a plate and shooed me toward the table. "Sit. Eat. You look like you're about to fall over."

"And here I thought I was doing so much better." I snagged a chair across from Alice and set the food on the table in front of me. "Maybe some coffee would help. I've slept a ton but still feel so tired."

"Having a building collapse on top of you is bound to do that to a person," Alice muttered, shaking her head.

"You definitely deserve a cup of coffee after all that." Gemma set a full mug on the table. "Want creamer or sugar?"

I beamed her an appreciative smile. "Thanks, black is fine."

"You're welcome." She dropped onto the chair next to me. "Is Wrecker taking good care of you?"

"Mm-hmm."

I focused on my food to cover the fact that my cheeks were filling with heat, but it didn't work.

"That blush and the cut on your back are answer enough." Gemma giggled. "I think it's safe to assume he's taking excellent care of you."

"They all do." Alice patted her twins' heads. "And that's how so many of us end up pregnant."

My cheeks burned hotter—and not just because I

nearly choked on the bite I'd just taken. The memory of Reid's words from the night before bounced around in my mind. Luckily, Alice and Gemma didn't push further, letting me finish breakfast instead.

After I was done, I tried to help clear a few plates before Alice shooed me away. I was still sipping my coffee when Blade walked into the kitchen, dressed in scrubs and looking like he hadn't slept much.

"Coffee hot?" he asked, already making a beeline for the pot.

"Yup," Gemma confirmed, nudging the half-full carafe toward him.

He poured a cup, then glanced my way with a tired nod. "Still doing okay?"

"Yeah," I confirmed with a small smile.

He grunted what might've been a "you're welcome" before leaning against the counter. His gaze flicked to Gemma and Alice before returning to me. "What's Wrecker up to?"

"I'm not sure what exactly." I shrugged. "Just that he's handling some club business."

Blade nodded. "It's good that he's keeping busy. This time of year is hard for him."

My brows drew together. "Why?"

Blade sighed. "Anniversary's coming up."

I waited, giving him space to decide whether he'd tell me more. He didn't.

It was Alice who spoke next, her voice gentler than before. "He's visited her both years I've known him. I'm sure it'll be the same now."

"Her?" My fingers twisted together as a sharp flicker of jealousy caught me off guard.

"He earned the name Wrecker for more than one reason." Blade crossed his arms over his chest. "We knew what he did during his time with Spec Ops in the military. He can turn a building into wreckage with precision unlike anyone else and also clear a path through it to save people nobody thought could be rescued."

My chest tightened as I nodded, remembering the strength in Reid's arms when he pulled me out. "I discovered that firsthand when he got to me faster than I thought possible."

"He's the best at what he does, but even Wrecker doesn't have a perfect record." Blade scrubbed his palm down his face. "Doesn't like talking about it, but Fox didn't give him a choice back when he was prospecting for us. Normally, he's stoic as fuck, but there were a couple of days when he was a wreck. Prez dug it outta him, how shit went sideways and he didn't get to a woman in time."

I pressed trembling fingers to my mouth with a gasp.

"She made it out of the rubble alive," he hurried to explain. "But all that time buried under concrete and steel left her legs beyond saving."

"And Reid blames himself for it," I whispered.

"Yup," Blade confirmed with a sharp nod. "He carries the weight of that woman spendin' her days in a wheelchair the same way he does the guys he knew over there who never made it back home. Even more, because he thinks if he'd just been a little faster, she'd have a normal life."

The weight of those words sank deep. I finally understood why he didn't like me thanking him for rescuing me. And the shadows that passed through his dark eyes. It was guilt he carried over memories of someone he hadn't been able to fully save.

Blinking quickly, I looked down at my lap as I wondered how I could help Reid heal from something like this.

"But now he has you," Gemma pointed out, almost as though she had read my mind.

Straightening my spine, I nodded. "This year, he won't be alone during that visit."

Blade flashed me an approving smile. "That's how I know he'll be okay this time. Nothing better for a man than a good woman who stands by his side when things get rough."

"Aw, I'm gonna tell Elise that you can say sweet things even when she's not around," Alice teased, lightening the mood.

Deviant walked in and scowled at Blade. "You better not be sayin' sweet shit to my wife."

Alice rolled her eyes, completely unbothered by her husband's possessive tone. "Relax, he was just trying to reassure Peyton."

I smiled at their easy banter, but my thoughts were still tangled around what I'd learned.

"Good." Deviant's attention shifted to me. "I sent over another batch of files for Wrecker to look at later. Permits, building specs, contractor databases. If you're bored and want to dig in, knock yourself out."

"That would be great. I'll take a look right away," I promised.

"Laptop's still upstairs, right?" he asked.

I nodded.

"Perfect." He rounded the table to pick up one of the boys. "Let me know if you find anything."

"Will do," I confirmed with a smile that widened when his other son reached for him too.

After heading back to Reid's room, I opened the laptop and loaded the files Deviant mentioned.

Skimming through spreadsheets, I cross-referenced permit numbers and flagged discrepancies that didn't sit right.

It wasn't much. But at least I was doing something, which helped me feel useful instead of helpless. It was a way to help Reid.

If I could find a lead, maybe it would matter. Possibly even ease the shadows I'd seen in his eyes. Or at least not add to them.

11

WRECKER

I leaned over Midnight's desk, eyes locked on the large monitor set between us. Kane's face filled the left half of the display—jaw set, sunglasses pushed up on his forehead, his voice clipped and pissed. The other half streamed live from a helmet cam, giving me a gut-dropping view of twisted metal, shattered concrete, and dust-slick chaos. The entire side of the building looked like it'd folded in on itself, all crumpled steel and splintered wood, mangled by the force of the crash.

Kane controlled a racing empire in the south. Some legal and a whole lot more illegal. He'd established the Redline Kings MC a few years ago, but even before then, we'd been tight allies. Storm had known Kane longer than any of us, but over the years, he'd proven himself more than once. He wasn't a patch but still family.

"Driver lost control," Kane said, voice tight. "Tried to cut the inside on the last turn, went wide. Slammed straight into the fucking pit-side structure."

"Anyone inside?" I asked, scanning the cam feed. The guy wearing the helmet—one of Kane's crew—stepped over a slab of drywall and ducked beneath a dangling beam.

"Three on the roster. Mechanic, engineer, and one rookie tech. Can't raise any of 'em."

Midnight stood with his arms crossed beside me, silent but watching. I studied the shifting mess on-screen—weight distribution, entry points, pinch zones. Same shit I used to do with my crew back in the Army. You didn't get a second chance in a collapse. One wrong move, and the whole thing came down on your skull.

"Tell your guy to come around the left. That I-beam's load-bearing. Looks stable. Use it."

Kane relayed the instruction without question, trusting that I knew my shit and could save his guys.

"Yeah," I muttered as the crewman followed my directions, angling between a support column and a caved-in wall. "That's it. Get eyes in the back corner."

It took over an hour, but they pulled all three of the trapped men from the rubble. One with a broken leg, another knocked clean out, and the third dazed and coughing but alive. I exhaled hard and leaned back in my chair. My shoulders ached from the tension, and sweat had dried under my cut, making the leather stick to my neck.

"Appreciate the eyes, brother," Kane said, pulling his shades down. "Owe you one."

"Stack it," I said. "I'll call in the marker when it counts."

He grinned and killed the feed.

I was about to leave when my cell buzzed on the table. "Yeah."

Deviant didn't bother with hello. "You're gonna want to hear this."

I grunted—my version of "go ahead."

"Eclipse is circling the fucking drain," he said. "Their golden boy—Blackthorn Properties—is getting nailed with a class-action. Billion-dollar lawsuit, Wrecker. All those families from the collapse sites are coming for blood. And Eclipse? They underwrote all of it."

I let out a low whistle. "So if the buildings went down because of faulty materials..."

"They're on the hook for every cent," he

confirmed. "But here's the thing—if it's sabotage? If someone made those buildings fall? Then Eclipse isn't responsible for the damages. Just owes a fat refund to Blackthorn."

"Which means Eclipse has motive to make those collapses look like someone else's fault."

"Exactly. And I'm positive they've been laying down bribes like fucking breadcrumbs. Two shell companies have been getting sizable transfers in the past six months. One's a front for whoever's acting as the state 'consultant' on the failure reports."

"And the other?" I asked, though I was beginning to formulate a suspicion.

He paused. "Still tracing it. But I have Peyton cross-referencing the timelines. If the pattern holds, three more structures haven't dropped yet."

"When's the court date?"

"Two weeks. If they're gonna make those buildings disappear, it's gotta be before then."

I scrubbed a hand through my hair, every muscle in my shoulders going tight again.

"Keep digging," I said. "I want names, faces, and fucking time stamps."

"Already on it. I'll update you soon."

I hung up and turned to Midnight, who was

already watching me with that expression he got when shit smelled worse than usual.

"Put someone on Blackthorn." We were already watching Eclipse. "I want eyes on every exec., every site. If anything fucking moves, I want to know before it happens."

He nodded. "I'll tap Storm and Wolf. You think we'll find evidence?"

"If we don't," I said, already pulling out my phone, "we better catch the bastards in the fucking act."

I made the calls—old favors, the kind that cost time and blood. A few of my engineering contacts were gonna sweep those three sites top to bottom. I wanted prints, fibers, residue. Anything they could get before the wrecking crew showed up. If there was no trail, we'd post guards and wait in the dark.

When the last call ended, I headed straight for the compound.

The moment I walked into my room, the scent hit me—cinnamon and vanilla. I was suddenly hungry. And not for the breakfast I hadn't eaten this morning.

Peyton was perched on the edge of the bed, legs crossed, her hair pulled into a messy bun. A manila folder sat in her lap, her fingers tapping against it like she couldn't wait another second.

The look on her face told me she'd found something.

"You won't believe this," she said, standing and holding out the file.

I took it, my fingers brushing hers as I flipped it open. Inside were printed screenshots, corporate filings, and a half-dozen profile shots—men in tactical gear, caught mid-step.

My blood turned to ice.

"The other shadow subsidiary getting the Eclipse transfers is a company run by guys from your old unit."

I stared at the image.

"That's Calder," I said, jaw locking.

The bastard who knew exactly how to drop a structure without anyone tracing the cause. I'd taught the motherfucker everything he knew.

"He's the one on all the footage," Peyton said softly. "The walk, the build, even the gloves."

I nodded once, tight and grim.

She stepped closer, voice barely above a whisper. "What are we gonna do?"

I stared at her for a beat—at the worry creasing

her brow, the fury simmering behind those violet eyes. She wasn't scared. She was ready to go to war.

But that had to wait. And when the time came, she wouldn't be anywhere near the battlefield.

"We'll handle it later," I said, tossing the file on the desk.

Her lips parted in confusion. "But—"

I grabbed the front of her shirt and yanked her into me, her body colliding with mine, fitting just right because she fucking belonged there. "Right now," I said, voice dropping, "we have more important matters."

Then I crushed my mouth to hers.

She melted against me, breath hitching, fingers gripping my sides like she couldn't stand even an inch of space between us.

Later, we'd hunt Calder. We'd burn his world to ash.

But tonight?

Tonight, she was mine.

12

PEYTON

I wasn't sure how much progress the Iron Rogues had made since I traced that shell company back to Wrecker's old unit. The moment Reid saw Ward Calder's name tied to it, the pieces started falling into place—but not the way I expected. It was personal now. More than just structural negligence or corporate greed.

Reid hadn't told me everything, but I knew they were moving fast behind the scenes. He promised they had it handled. And I believed him.

Which was why I hadn't pushed for more details. Especially not over the past couple of days.

What Blade had shared with me still echoed in my head, allowing me to better understand the weight Reid carried, and the shadows in his eyes.

It was also how I could guess where he was headed even before he confirmed it.

"I need to take care of something. Not sure when I'll get back, but I'll be gone for a while," he told me, his voice quieter than usual as he grabbed his keys from the top of the dresser.

I stood and crossed the room, my heart hammering. "And I'm coming with you."

My firm tone got his attention. His gaze locked on mine. "You don't even know where I'm going, baby."

"I know about the woman you feel like you let down." I reached up, resting my hand against his chest. "And how you visit her each year."

His jaw flexed. "How'd you know?"

"Blade told me." Irritation flashed in his dark gaze, and I hurried to explain. "Only because I got all jealous when Alice said something about you going to see her."

One side of his mouth kicked up. "You got possessive over me?"

"Yeah." I tugged on his cut as I went on my toes to give him a quick kiss. "Which is why Blade took pity on me and shared the story of how you got your road name."

"You don't need to worry about Susan."

"I know, but I still want to come with you." I smiled up at him. "Let me support you like you do with me."

A long pause stretched between us, his body still but his thoughts warring behind those dark eyes. Finally, he gave a short nod. "Okay."

The hour-long drive passed mostly in silence, but not the kind that felt awkward. We took his truck, and Reid's fingers stayed wrapped around mine on the center console, his thumb tracing idle strokes over my skin. He didn't speak much, and I didn't ask him to. I was at his side, and that was enough for me.

When we pulled into a quiet neighborhood on the outskirts of Chattanooga, I was happy to see how normal the house looked. It was small but warm-looking, painted a soft blue with white shutters and flowers blooming in containers near the porch. A welcome mat sat at the bottom of a long ramp that led to the front door.

Reid cut the engine and sat there for a second, staring at the house like it held ghosts.

"Ready?" I asked gently.

His voice was rough as he answered, "More than I usually am."

The woman who answered the door was tiny, but there was nothing hesitant in the way she moved.

She rolled herself smoothly back to make room for us, smiling as though she hadn't noticed the pain in Reid's eyes.

"Hey, stranger," she said softly.

Reid stepped forward and bent to wrap her in a hug. "Hey, Susan."

The way her arms came around his shoulders made my throat tighten. There was no awkwardness between them. Just understanding.

When they pulled apart, her gaze shifted to me. "And you brought a guest for the first time ever."

Reid slid his arm around my waist. "This is my Peyton."

"Anyone who's important to Reid is more than welcome in my home." Susan offered her hand with a warm smile. "It's nice to meet you."

She led us into the living room, and I caught glimpses of framed photos along the walls. My eyes widened when I realized one of them was from her wedding, and she was in her wheelchair at the altar.

Susan easily transferred to the couch, her balance so natural that it was as if her chair had never been anything but a part of her life. She looked comfortable and happy, but there was still an almost tortured look in Reid's eyes as he watched her.

I reached for his hand, lacing my fingers with his.

He didn't let go. Not even when the front door opened behind us and a tall, handsome man stepped in, carrying a grocery bag.

"Babe, they were out of the herbal tea you love, so I got the next best one. Oh, I thought I'd beat you here."

His smile was easy, but the moment his eyes landed on Susan, something shifted. The way he looked at her—like the sun rose and set with his wife—made something ache in my chest. He walked over and kissed her forehead before lowering a hand gently to her stomach.

I saw the way Susan flushed, her hand covering his, and I gasped.

Reid went still beside me.

"We were going to wait a little longer before telling anyone," Susan admitted with a bashful grin. "But it seems so fitting that you're the first to know."

"You're pregnant?" I asked, my voice catching on a thread of emotion.

She nodded, glowing now. "Yeah. Due right around Thanksgiving."

I glanced at Reid, but he wasn't smiling. Not yet. The guilt was still there, carved into every line of his face. As though seeing her happy somehow deepened his remorse.

"We have even more to be thankful for this year." Her husband shot Reid a smile. "Because of you."

Reid looked uncomfortable with his gratitude, shrugging it off.

Susan shot him an exasperated look before she asked, "Can I steal Peyton for a second?"

"Sure," Reid replied.

She transferred back to her chair, then her husband dropped the bag onto her lap, and she motioned me to follow her as she rolled toward the kitchen.

When we stopped near the fridge, Susan took my hand.

"I know that look," she said softly. "You're worried about him."

"I want him to stop hurting." My voice cracked. "And not just because he saved me too."

She shook her head with a deep sigh. "He doesn't see it, but Reid gave me back a life that turned out even better than I ever dreamed."

"I wish he saw it that way."

She squeezed my fingers. "Now it's your turn to save him, Peyton. You have to be the one to pull him out of the emotional rubble he buried himself in."

My throat closed, but I nodded. "I will."

After helping her put away the groceries and

make a pot of herbal tea for us and coffee for the guys, I followed Susan back into the living room.

We chatted for a little while, mostly Susan sharing what had been going on in her life besides her big news. When her husband was in the kitchen, putting our mugs in the sink, her hand drifted to her stomach. "We decided that if it's a boy, we're naming him Reid."

He froze, the impact of her words hitting someplace deep.

"Don't argue with me," Susan added with a smile. "It's already decided. And not because you owe me anything, but because you don't. You gave me this life, and I wouldn't change a single part of it."

Reid didn't speak, but I saw the change in his expression. How the sharp edges softened, even if just for a moment. Getting to his feet, he leaned down and hugged her again, holding her tighter this time.

We said our goodbyes not long after, and the drive back to Old Bridge passed in quiet comfort. His hand found mine again, resting between us on the console like it belonged there. Because it did.

I kept thinking about Susan's words and the way Reid had looked at her when she told him about the baby. There was so much pain still buried inside him, but I saw something else too—a flicker of peace. Maybe even hope.

The late afternoon sun dipped lower as we turned onto the familiar road leading to the Iron Rogues compound. Reid eased the truck past the gates, and I glanced over at him with a teasing smile.

"I guess Reid Jr. isn't a possibility for us if Susan already claimed the name."

His knuckles whitened around the wheel. "Us?"

"Hypothetically. Someday." My cheeks filled with heat as I remembered how he'd taken me without anything between us. And how often he talked about filling me up with his come. "Maybe sooner than later, considering you haven't used a single condom any of the times we've had sex."

A low growl rumbled from his chest, and his hand slid from the console to my thigh, fingers gripping with unmistakable possession.

"Damn fucking straight." A sensual shiver raced down my spine as the truck rolled to a stop. "And when I get you back to my room, I'm gonna do it again."

13

PEYTON

A few of the guys and their old ladies were hanging out in the lounge area of the clubhouse when Reid practically dragged me into the building. I didn't miss their smirks when he ignored their greetings, and the laughter as he tossed me over his shoulder and growled, "You're movin' too slow, baby."

Hanging upside down over his shoulder, I gave Gemma a little wave while we passed her. My lips curved into a satisfied smile when she murmured, "Guess you guys don't need to worry about Wrecker being in a bad mood today."

"Finally found the woman who brings him peace," Hawk agreed.

My smile was huge when Reid finally dropped me on the bed.

"You look like the cat that ate the canary, baby," he drawled as he slid his cut off his shoulders and hung it off the back of his chair.

Giggling, I teased, "Does that mean you want to eat my pussy to make us even?"

"Always," he growled.

My inner walls clenched at the heat in his dark eyes. I scrambled to my knees to strip out of my clothes while Reid did the same. Now that my shoulder was fully healed, he'd stopped holding back out of fear of causing me pain. I loved that I could make him lose control now. Knowing I could unravel him like that was a rush.

"I need you so much, please."

My soft confession made Reid move even faster. He shoved his jeans down his legs and kicked them off, along with his boxer briefs. Then he crawled on the mattress like a feral beast ready to claim his mate. Pressing me into the mattress, he cupped my cheek with one hand while balancing the rest of his weight with the other.

Dipping his head, he captured my lips in a deep kiss that left me breathless. His hard-on pressed against my core, but he took his time, our tongues tangling as our lips slid together.

He lifted his head, but I wasn't ready for the kiss to end and whimpered, "Please don't stop."

I had been a little uncertain our first time together when Reid had told me to beg, but I was so happy I hadn't balked at doing it because I quickly discovered that I loved his reaction each time I panted, "Please."

"I fucking love how you beg so sweetly, baby," he rasped before giving me what I wanted.

Reid growled low in his throat and crushed his mouth against mine again. Nothing was gentle about this kiss. My plea had shattered the last thread of his restraint. He gave me more of his weight until there wasn't a breath of space between us.

My lips parted for him, and I met his hunger with my own, not holding back either. It didn't matter how fast this was moving—I needed Reid. And not just his kisses...I wanted all of him.

Twining my arms around his neck, I circled his waist with my legs. With the change in position, his hard length slipped between my drenched folds, making him groan. "You're already so damn wet for me."

"Because I need you, Reid." I bucked my hips off the mattress. "Please."

"Gonna eat your pretty pussy first, then I'll give you my cock."

"Yes," I gasped as he gripped my thigh to widen my legs.

His lips trailed over my heated skin, teeth nibbling at the underside of my breast before he caught my pebbled nipple and tugged.

"Reid," I whimpered, raking my fingers through his hair.

He swirled his tongue around my nipple, making the peak harden more when the cool air hit it. "Want to hear you say my name like that when you come for me, baby."

He shuffled back to lie down between my legs, perching my thighs on his shoulders. Then he nipped at the soft skin of my inner thigh, all the way up until he lapped at my center. He swirled his tongue around my clit before dipping lower to thrust it inside me, building my pleasure with a skill that showed he'd been paying close attention to my reactions each time we'd been in bed together.

My nails dug into his scalp. "Oh yes! Please. I need more. That feels so good."

He devoured me like a starving man, pushing me higher until I felt as though I was about to fly apart into a million pieces.

"Come for me. Now," he demanded, pinching my clit.

Fireworks exploded behind my eyelids, the pleasure almost more than I could bear. "Yes! Oh yes, Reid!"

He didn't let up, eating me through my orgasm and making it last even longer. It was a good thing I was already in bed because my body practically melted into the mattress by the time the last wave of my release crashed over me.

Reid crawled on top of me again, his dick even harder than before. Lowering his head, he captured my mouth once more. His hips were cradled between my thighs, and a deep groan rumbled up his chest.

Rocking forward, he slid his hard length through my wetness before notching the tip at my entrance. Inching inside, he nipped my bottom lip. They parted, and our tongues tangled together as he punched his hips forward until he was anchored deep inside me.

We'd had more sex than I thought was possible since he took my virginity, but his thick dick still stretched my pussy enough to sting a little on that first thrust.

"You feel that, baby?" he rasped, circling his hips. "Your sweet pussy was made to take my cock. The only one it'll ever be wrapped around like this."

We hadn't talked about the future, but when he said stuff like that in the heat of the moment, I couldn't help but hope he really meant it. Especially since there wasn't anything between us.

With as much come as he'd pumped inside me, I was bound to get pregnant sooner than later. Especially since he seemed to be on a mission to make it happen. And even though I'd been too focused on school to think about falling in love and building a family, meeting Reid had changed all that. Shifted my priorities in a way I'd never expected, which was part of why I hadn't hesitated to let my professors know I had an emergency and wouldn't be in class this week. I still wanted to finish my degree, but I also wanted to make space for a life. With him.

My thoughts scattered when he gripped my jaw and tilted my head back to kiss me again. And then I completely lost the ability to think when his dick dragged against my inner walls, sending sparks of pleasure through my body before he thrust back inside.

"Is that what you needed, baby?" he grunted, his dark eyes filled with heat as they met mine.

"Yes," I gasped, clutching at his shoulders. "More, please."

"Such a good girl, begging me for what you need," he grunted, picking up the pace. "Even when you know damn well I'm always gonna give it to you. No chance in hell I'm not gonna to sink my cock inside your tight pussy every chance I get."

He pulled out until only the tip of his dick was still inside me, and then he snapped his hips forward again, filling me until his balls slapped against my butt cheeks. Over and over again, while I held on for the ride.

Although I'd already had a huge orgasm, my pleasure quickly began to climb again. Then it got even better when he hiked my legs up to press my knees against my chest.

He was able to slide in even deeper in this position, and it only took a few more thrusts before I flew apart, my orgasm stronger than the first. "Reid! Yes!"

"That's it, baby. Come for me while you take every fucking inch of my cock and milk my come."

His dirty talk intensified my pleasure, and so did the splash of his release against my inner walls when he followed me into the abyss.

I was out of breath when he rolled to his side, taking me with him, his dick still inside me.

Today had been a big day. Going with Reid to meet Susan had brought us even closer. And cuddling with him like this after mind-blowing sex only reinforced that feeling.

14

WRECKER

The morning was soft and quiet. Faint light spilled across the sheets, slanting through the blinds in bars that painted Peyton's bare back in pale gold.

She was draped over me, naked and warm. Her limbs tangled up with mine, her face tucked into my throat, and her leg thrown over my hip like she was trying to fuse us. Her dark lashes flickered slightly, like her dreams were shifting.

I didn't want to move. Not even to breathe too deeply in case it pulled me out of the moment. Would've stayed in it forever if I could.

My hand rested on her thigh, fingers spread possessively over smooth skin that still bore the marks from where I'd gripped her hours ago. My come had dried between them, and I'd be lying if I said I didn't like knowing it was still there. Soaked into her skin like a brand.

She murmured something against my chest, then snuggled closer, soft and content. With my other hand, I stroked her back with slow, possessive sweeps, my fingers drifting lower each time until they cupped the curve of her ass. I didn't even get to enjoy the moment before my phone buzzed on the nightstand.

"Fucking hell," I growled, reaching for it and squinting at the screen. Midnight.

I answered with a grunt, voice still full of gravel. "What?"

"We've got a situation." Midnight's voice was clipped, tight. "One of our surveillance teams at the Stonegate site ran a sweep an hour ago. Found it rigged to blow. Whole fucking condo building's wired."

"Fuck me." I sat up fast enough to jostle Peyton. She blinked, head lifting slightly, frowning when I pulled away. I mouthed an apology and caressed her cheek, making her smile and settle back against the pillows.

"They didn't see that shit before?" I muttered into the phone, scrubbing a hand down my face.

"They're pissed about it, too. Think Calder's crew slipped in during a shift change yesterday. Used the cover to plant the charges."

I swung my legs over the side of the bed and stood. "Tell 'em not to beat themselves up. That team's good, but unless you're there to be the wrecking ball, trained demo crews can ghost in and out. Especially ones taught by me."

Midnight spoke again. "Wrecker, there's a fucking timer."

My jaw clenched. "How long?"

"Four hours," Midnight replied. "Ticking down fast. They spotted it less than ten minutes ago."

"Meet me at Iron Shield in thirty. I'll grab my gear." I hung up and turned to Peyton.

She pushed up onto one elbow, sheets slipping down her chest. Her hair was a mess, her cheeks flushed with sleep, and her lips kiss-swollen from last night. She looked soft, warm, like every man's fantasy. And I was about to leave her in a cold fucking bed.

"What's wrong?" she asked, voice husky.

"Condo building's wired," I said, pulling on my jeans. "Midnight's guys spotted the charges this morning. I gotta go check it out."

"I'm coming," she said immediately, scooting to the edge of the bed.

"No, the fuck you're not," I fired back as I reached for my shirt.

"Yes, I am," she snapped, eyes flashing. "We both know how to identify the patterns in the setups. I've seen the documents, and I've been on those sites. I can help."

"No," I said, voice hard. "Not up for discussion."

Her spine straightened. "Reid—"

I finally stopped and spun around to face her. "Not a chance in hell. That building's set to blow. We don't know if someone's still inside, or if it's rigged with a manual detonation that they'll press as soon as they fucking see you. You're not stepping foot near that shit."

She stood, stark naked, arms crossed over her chest, and her eyes sparking with heat and fire. "Do we have to have this argument again? I'm not made of freaking glass!"

"No," I growled, stalking closer until I crowded her, and she had to tilt her head back to meet my eyes. "You're made of fire, and steel, and soft fucking curves I want wrapped around me till the end of the fucking world. You might not be made of glass, but you're mine to protect. Which is exactly why I'm not letting you anywhere near an active bomb site!"

Her lips parted, outrage rising, but I leaned in close and dropped my voice.

"You could be pregnant, Peyton."

That shut her up. Her breath caught, eyes wide. Color rushed into her cheeks. Then her jaw worked for a beat before she muttered, "Low blow."

"Maybe," I said, brushing my knuckles down her jaw. "But I'll take every dirty advantage I have if it keeps you breathing."

Her nostrils flared as she stared at me, then she huffed and looked away. "Are you trying to knock me up just so you can wrap me in a bubble?"

I smirked and bent to kiss the corner of her mouth. "No, baby. That's just a side perk."

She growled and shoved at my chest, but it was weak and halfhearted. "Jerk."

"I know." I shrugged on my shirt, then my cut.

She rolled her eyes but stepped forward, wrapping her arms around my waist. "You better come back to me, Reid."

I tipped her chin up, kissed her hard, then pulled away with reluctance clawing at my chest.

"Be good," I rasped. "And don't leave the room

unless you're wearing my cut." After kissing her hard and fast, I whispered, "Be back before you miss me."

I cupped the back of her head for one more beat, then forced myself to leave before I dragged her back into bed and said fuck the building.

THE SITE WAS ALREADY roped off when Midnight and I rolled up on our bikes, parking a good distance away, just in case. One of his trucks was backed toward the entrance, and two of his guys were standing guard. They'd secured the perimeter, but I could tell by their grim expressions that the unease was already setting in. Timers had a way of fucking with your head.

Three more brothers pulled up, parking their hogs beside ours before joining us.

"Place was condemned last year," Midnight muttered as we moved toward the busted entrance. "Inspector's report said that shifts in the ground had caused the foundation to become uneven."

"Fifty bucks says that asshole set up an offshore bank account right before the report was published," Wolf commented dryly.

"Not taking that bet," Midnight grunted before continuing. "Rather than spend the money to tear it down, they let it sit."

"And with the lawsuit, they risk a new inspection shedding light on the shitty build," I surmised.

Inside, the air was stale and smelled like mold and decay. Carpets were pulled up in strips, and everything was covered in dust thick enough to coat your lungs. The floors creaked as we moved quietly, our flashlights slicing through the darkness where the sunlight couldn't reach.

My gaze scanned everything. We went unit by unit, making note of any charges we found so that our crew could work on dismantling them.

On the east side of the third floor, in what used to be a property manager's office, I spotted a rolled tube of paper jammed against the back leg of an old, rusted desk.

"What the hell's that?" Wolf muttered.

I crouched, snatched the cylinder, and tipped it so the papers inside slipped out. Then I unrolled them on a half-collapsed couch. The blood in my veins turned to acid. "What the fuck?"

They were old training schematics. Diagrams I'd created back in the service—test scenarios, practice plans. Where to plant charges. What angles to use for max impact. My name was scrawled on the bottom corner of each one. It was *my* fucking playbook.

"Those sons of bitches," I muttered.

"What is it?" Midnight asked.

"They've been using my old plans. My techniques. Copying every fucking thing I ever taught them." My voice was low, lethal. "That's why these buildings are falling so clean."

"You think Calder's crew stole your shit?"

"I know they did."

Ward Calder didn't have to say a word.

I felt him walk in.

"Well, well," a voice drawled from the doorway. "Didn't expect to see you here without your little shadow."

I turned slowly, and there he was. Standing with that smug fucking face, holding a detonator in one hand. "Shame. I was hoping she'd be here. Would've made the boom even more worth it. Kill two birds with...well, you get the metaphor."

"You sick fuck," I snarled, stepping forward.

"Don't get noble now, Owens." He waved his other hand and flicked a button, initiating a deadman's switch, now clutched in his grip. "Step back," he said, eyes wild. "Try anything, and we all go up in a fucking fireball."

"You suicidal now, Calder?" I asked, low. "Not your usual style."

"I know you found the payouts," he hissed. "The trail. My name on that shell company. I'm a dead man walking once that shit hits the media."

Midnight shifted beside me, fingers twitching near his weapon. I gave a slight shake of my head. Calder was wired. One twitch, and he'd take the whole place with him.

Then another voice cut through the tension like a slow drag of a blade across a throat. "Well, shit. Y'all started the party without me?"

Kane's voice echoed through the broken hallway like a goddamn movie entrance. He strolled in as though he had all the time in the world, dark shades tucked into his half-buttoned shirt, like he'd just rolled out of bed and grabbed the first set of clothes he saw. Two of his men hovered behind him, weapons drawn.

Calder flinched and turned toward the sound, distracted for half a breath.

It was all I needed.

I lunged.

We crashed into the desk with a bang, rolling it across cracked linoleum as I fought for the switch. My fist smashed into his jaw. He hit my shoulder, so I slammed him into the ground hard, and the detonator skittered away. He shouted with fury as his elbow cracked against my temple. I took the hit and grabbed for the deadman switch.

He fought like he had nothing left to lose—wild, fast, and dirty. But I was bigger, stronger, had trained longer, and I was a fuck of a lot meaner. I got the switch away from him and twisted the device hard until it snapped.

Then I clocked him in the jaw and let him drop.

Kane crouched beside me, one brow raised. "Looked like you had it handled."

I blew out a breath and wiped blood off my brow. "Then why the fuck are you here?"

He grinned as he got to his feet and grasped my hand, pulling up next to him.

"Ran into Deviant at the compound," he said with a shrug. "Said you might need backup. Figured I'd stop by before talking to Fox about borrowing Racer."

Before I could reply, the door banged open, and two more men stormed in. Faces I knew too well.

"Fuck," I muttered. Talbot and Lang were both from my old unit.

Fucking traitors.

They saw Calder crumpled on the floor and charged toward us.

Kane and I moved fast, meeting them halfway. It was brutal. Fists and boots connecting with muscle and bone. I took a punch to the ribs that cracked something loose, but I got Talbot in a chokehold and didn't let go until he blacked out.

Kane fought like a pitbull in a bar brawl. Lang only got in one hit before Kane slammed him into the wall hard enough to make the drywall crack.

The fight wasn't clean, but it was fast. In five minutes, both were tied up, bruised, and bleeding next to Calder.

I checked my watch. "Fuck. We have less than thirty minutes left."

I grabbed my radio. "We're outta time. Pull the crew. Get the hell out."

"Copy."

Wolf jogged into the room, breath short. "Truck's ready."

"Take Calder," I ordered. "Get him loaded up."

Wolf nodded, grabbed the unconscious bastard by the collar, and started dragging.

Kane jerked one of the still-struggling assholes to his feet, and I did the same with the other. Then we let them out into the hallway and headed toward the lobby.

The floor vibrated beneath our boots as we took the stairs down. I didn't like the way it felt.

"This doesn't count as a favor," I muttered to Kane when we reached the first floor.

A sudden beep pierced the air.

My head snapped down. Talbot was wearing a watch—and it was blinking red.

My stomach dropped. "Shit—"

I didn't get to finish.

The explosion was deafening.

Pain slammed into my side like a truck. The world spun, then blinked out completely.

When I came to, everything hurt.

Pain burned in my ribs, my thigh, and my fucking skull. My ears rang like a motherfucker. I sucked in a breath, and my lungs burned as though they'd been scrubbed raw with gravel.

A shadow blocked the light.

Kane.

He was crouched over me, bruised and filthy but grinning.

"How about now?" he asked, voice smug.

"Fuck you," I rasped.

He laughed and offered me a hand. "You're welcome."

15

WRECKER

The room didn't look like much.

From the outside, it was all angles and shadows. Just a squat, windowless structure tucked into the thick tree line at the very back of the Iron Rogues compound. The kind of place even the brothers didn't talk about unless they needed to. There was no sign. No path. If you didn't know the building existed, you'd walk right past it.

If you did know, you damn well better be on the right side of the club before you crossed its threshold.

Inside, the air was always cool. Sterile. Like bleach and blood had seeped into the bones of the place and never left. The lighting was harsh by design. Nowhere to hide in the shadows of a room meant for tearing truths out of liars.

It had several rooms. Two cells with reinforced doors and shackles bolted to the walls. Two rooms built for interrogation—both soundproof, lined in steel and tile, with a drain in the center of the floor, making for easy cleanup.

That was where we were keeping Calder.

The small kitchenette mostly existed to hose shit off—knives, hands, boots. And a lounge of sorts with beaten leather chairs, battered lockers, and a scarred table with a few half-used decks of cards and a bottle of whiskey that no one ever touched unless something needed burning.

And then there was the tool "closet."

Hidden behind a set of double doors was a grid of shelves and hooks packed with everything from bone saws to jumper cables. More surgical than sadistic, but that didn't make it any prettier.

When I stepped into the interrogation room, Calder was zip-tied to the chair, ankles bound to the floor. The bastard had a split lip and a bloodied nose, but he was breathing just fine. The boys who brought him here knew better than to rough him up too much. We needed answers and getting them would be the best way for me to release all the pent-up fury before I went home to Peyton.

I shut the door behind me and let the latch click into place.

Calder looked up, and when he saw the expression on my face, I saw the flicker in his eyes. Panic. He knew what happened to men in rooms like these. But he tried to hide it.

"Come to finish the job, Owens?" he rasped, lips cracked and red.

"No," I said, voice flat. "Not yet."

I dragged a chair across the floor, the sound sharp and deliberate, then sat down in front of him, elbows on my knees.

"I have questions."

"Go fuck yourself," he spat, bloody saliva landing on my boot.

I smiled.

There was no rush, so I took my time with him. By the time I stepped back out into the hallway, the towel in my hand was half red. My knuckles were raw. My shirt was sticking to my chest, damp with a mix of sweat and someone else's blood. Calder wasn't dead— but he wasn't feeling like much of a man anymore.

Maverick leaned against the wall, arms crossed over his broad chest like he'd been there for a while. His eyes flicked to the towel, then back to my face.

"You kill him?" he asked, voice dry.

"Not yet," I muttered, heading straight for the sink in the kitchenette.

The water ran hot. I watched the blood swirl down the drain in rust-colored ribbons while I scrubbed my hands, the sting of soap biting into the splits in my skin.

"He talk?" Maverick asked.

I nodded once. "Gave it all up. Names, contacts. The rest of his crew. Every exec. connected to the developer and the insurance company. Gutted the whole fucking mess for me."

He let out a breath, low and tight. "Good. That'll help Fox and Stone build the case for exposure."

I shut off the tap and dried my hands with a clean towel, tossing the bloody one into the bin beneath the counter.

Maverick pushed off the wall and walked over, handing me a folded bundle of clothes—black tee, clean jeans, and my cut. I'd taken it off so it wouldn't be stained with blood or any other substances.

"Change before you head home. You smell like a murder scene."

I arched a brow. "Wasn't one."

"Yet," he said with a smirk.

I peeled off my shirt and dragged the clean one

over my head. My ribs protested, still sore from the blast. I wasn't gonna complain, though. I'd earned every bruise.

"Deviant figure out the money trail?" I asked, tugging on my vest.

"Yeah," Maverick said, tone going sharp. "It's a fuckin' shell game. Eclipse Insurance and the real estate group both trace back to the same parent company. So every time they 'paid out' for damages, they just moved the money from one pocket to the other."

"Slick," I muttered. "Bet they thought they were really clever."

"They did. Until you and Peyton started tugging at the seams."

At the mention of her name, my jaw clenched. I could still feel her hands on me from that morning. Heard her whispering my name when I kissed her goodbye. Smelled her skin under my palms. I hadn't liked leaving her alone, even locked up safely at the compound.

I suddenly noticed that Maverick had gone quiet, and the air was filled with tension.

Glancing over, I scowled.

He had that look—like he wanted to say something but knew I wasn't gonna like it.

"You're not gonna let me kill him, are you?"

Maverick's sigh was slow and reluctant.

"No. Fox and Stone agreed—if we kill Calder now, it could screw everything. His disappearance would raise too many flags when the media starts picking up what we're about to leak. The others might try to use him as a scapegoat and say he acted alone. We need him alive long enough to be exposed with the rest of the bastards."

I didn't reply right away.

My fists clenched, but I tried to reason with myself. Killing Calder would've been clean. Easy. One bullet. Done. But this wasn't about easy. It was about ensuring the entire rotten empire crumbled. And even I couldn't argue with some things.

"You're right," I said after a beat, the admission coming out like I'd eaten razor blades. "But I still wanna break his fucking spine."

Maverick clapped a hand on my shoulder. "Save it for after the trial."

I snorted. "That the plan? Let the court system handle it?"

He grinned. "Nah. We're just waiting till the right eyes see the evidence. Then he's all yours."

That was something, at least.

He tipped his chin toward the door. "Go home to your girl. You look like shit."

I gave a humorless laugh. "Feel like it too."

"Seriously," he said, stepping back. "Put this behind you for now. Give her the vest. Put a ring on her finger. Knock her up."

I smirked. "Already got a head start on that last part."

Maverick barked a laugh. "Wouldn't be a true Iron Rogue if you hadn't."

As I grabbed my keys and started toward the exit, I paused by the heavy steel door that led back to Calder's room. My hand tightened around the frame for a second, the urge to go back in and finish what I started riding me hard.

But I made myself walk away.

Because they were all right.

But that wasn't what got my feet moving. It was knowing my woman was waiting for me.

The second I stepped through the clubhouse doors, I barely had time to shut them before a blur of black curls and soft limbs crashed into my chest.

Peyton.

She launched herself at me and wrapped her arms tightly around my neck, her whole body vibrating with relief. I caught her easily—like I'd been waiting to hold her again since the second I left.

Which I fucking had.

I crushed my mouth to hers before a single word could pass between us. Her lips were soft and frantic, kissing me like I was air and she'd been choking without it. I licked deep, groaning into her mouth, my hands locking tight under her ass as I lifted her. Her legs wrapped around my waist, and for a heartbeat, nothing existed except her breath in my mouth and the desperate way she held on.

I knew there were others around, but at that moment, I didn't give a fuck.

She was mine. And they knew it.

However, I wasn't willing to let them see any more. I started down the hall, already headed toward our room, carrying her while she clung to me, breathless and so damn perfect. Her arms cinched tighter around me, her nose tucked into my neck like she needed to feel my pulse against her cheek to believe I was really back.

Then Fox's voice cut through the air.

"Wrecker."

He didn't shout, but his tone was sharp as a blade. That quiet, authoritative rasp that made it clear he expected obedience the first time he spoke.

I stopped mid-step, jaw grinding, holding back the snarl that threatened to snap loose. Peyton blinked at me, a little dazed from the kiss, eyes shining as she looked up.

I didn't want to let her go. Didn't want to fucking stop. But I'd given Fox my oath, and I would not defy him—unless he ever got between Peyton and me.

Forcing myself to breathe through the slow burn of frustration crawling down my spine, I turned.

Fox stood by the pool table, one brow raised, mouth tugged into a smug half smile. With a casual flick of his wrist, he tossed something my way.

I caught it without thinking.

The leather was soft and broken in. Smaller than mine, but unmistakable.

A black vest, tailored for a woman's frame. I knew that on the back was an Iron Rogues patch. And stitched across it would be the words: Property of Wrecker.

My chest clenched.

"'Bout fucking time," Fox said with a wink, then turned and walked off.

I grunted my thanks—though it sounded more like a growl—then turned back down the hallway, stalking toward our room with my woman still wrapped around me and my property patch clutched in one hand like it was a lifeline.

When I kicked the door shut behind us and set her on her feet, she swayed a little, cheeks flushed, lips kiss swollen. Her eyes dropped to the vest in my hand, going wide and shining like sunlight through amethyst.

But when I didn't move, the light dimmed.

I saw it—saw the flicker of doubt crease her brow, her teeth catching her bottom lip. She wanted to ask. I knew it.

The moment stretched too long, and she lost her nerve. A pout formed on her mouth, just a faint one, but it made me want to fucking devour her.

Biting back a grin, I couldn't help teasing her. She was just too damn cute.

Instead of explaining, I reached for my woman and slowly peeled her out of her clothes. Almost reverently. I'd waited for this since the moment I first laid eyes on her. My fingers brushed over her skin with possessive strokes, baring inch after perfect inch until she stood naked in front of me, flushed and gorgeous and mine.

Peyton watched my every move, and her breath caught when I set the vest aside, folding it carefully on the edge of the bed.

The pout was back, and fuck, it was adorable.

Finally, I picked up the cut again, circling her slowly like a wolf stalking its mate. Her eyes followed me as I came around behind her, dragging my fingertips along her spine.

I reached up and brushed her hair aside, leaning in close until my lips were at her ear.

"I love you," I rasped. "More than anything in the whole fucking world, Peyton. You were made to belong to me. And you're gonna be my old lady."

She sniffled softly, and her voice shook. "I love you too...so much."

I slid the vest onto her shoulders, easing her arms through the holes. When I smoothed it into place, staring at the large, bold patch, I nearly fucking lost it.

Because it was perfect.

That vest on her bare skin? My brand on her back?

Fuck. Me.

"Turn around, baby."

When she obeyed, my gaze roamed over her, from her pretty violet eyes to her tits playing peek-aboo with the leather to the sweet spot between her thighs and all the way down to her purple-tipped toes. When my gaze returned to her face, I twirled my finger, indicating that I wanted her to turn around again.

When she did, I stepped in behind her, unable to help myself.

"You have no idea what this does to me," I growled, wrapping my arms around her waist and hauling her back against my chest.

She gasped, hips rolling involuntarily as my hands slid up under the leather. I palmed her breasts, groaning when her nipples pebbled beneath my fingers.

"Seeing you like this," I whispered in her ear. "Wearing my brand like the perfect little prize you are. It makes me hard as fuck."

Peyton whimpered when I pinched her nipples between my fingers, twisting and plucking until her legs wobbled. "You like that, baby?"

"Yes," she gasped. "Please."

"I can smell how fucking wet you are," I rumbled. "Just from me playing with these incredible tits. Having my brand on your back."

I dragged one hand down and slipped it between her legs. My fingers slid through her soaked folds, and I cursed under my breath.

"Fuck, baby. You're drenched."

I pulled my hand up and sucked my fingers into my mouth, moaning like she was my last meal.

"Taste like heaven," I growled. "I'm gonna eat you till you scream."

"Yesss," she hissed.

"But first..."

She let out an adorable little growl when I grabbed her hips and steered her toward the desk.

"Patience," I murmured with a chuckle.

When we reached it, she glanced back at me, dazed and aroused. I smiled and popped open the drawer.

Her eyes widened when she saw the little black box.

"Reid..."

I opened it, revealing a slim, platinum ring with a two-carat diamond. It was simple, but strong and permanent.

"The only thing that would make this look better is a ring on your finger," I murmured, sliding it onto her delicate hand, "and a belly full of my kid."

She gasped as she held up her hand, then she turned her head to look at me with tears springing fresh in her eyes. I caught her mouth in a kiss, sealing the promise with my lips, then turned her around slowly before walking her back to the bed.

She shivered at the dark promise in my expression. By the time her knees hit the edge of the mattress, she was already falling back, panting, eyes wide with need.

I loomed over her, dragging the vest open to bare her chest.

"Now," I growled, "I'm gonna work on that second part."

Her eyes widened, a soft sound catching in her throat as I grabbed her knees and shoved them apart, spreading her open beneath me. The vest still clung to her shoulders, the soft leather framing her flushed skin, her peaked nipples, her heaving tits.

Mine.

Every fucking inch of her.

"Look at you," I rasped, dragging my hand from her ankle up the soft, quivering inside of her thigh. "Laid out in my cut, your ring on your finger, that sweet little pussy already soaked for me."

She moaned, arching her back, then her breath hitched.

"I'm gonna fuck you so deep, baby," I growled, leaning in to nip her bottom lip. "You'll still be feelin' me tomorrow. Dripping with my come."

Her lips parted as she gasped my name.

I kissed her again, hard and filthy, tongues tangling while I lined myself up and dragged the head of my cock through her slick opening. The second I nudged against her entrance, her hips jerked, thighs clamping around me.

"Please," she whispered. "I need you."

I sank into her with a groan that turned into a full-body shudder.

She was so damn tight, hot, and completely drenched.

Fucking heaven.

Her head fell back as I stretched her, slow but steady, letting her feel every inch as I filled her from root to tip. Her nails dug into my shoulders, those pretty lips trembling as she whimpered with need.

"You feel that?" I gritted. "That's your pussy taking what's fucking hers. Because I'm yours, baby. You got that?"

The look in her eyes was wild, but she nodded.

I punched my hips forward. "You're mine now, baby. Fucking owned."

She cried out as I buried myself deep.

"Say it," I snarled, slamming into her again.

"I'm yours," she gasped. "Always yours—oh, yes! Yes—Reid!"

I fucked her hard, watching her tits bounce beneath me, the vest shifting as her body arched and twisted. Dipping down, I sucked a nipple into my mouth, and she shuddered, her pussy clamping hard around me. Then I switched sides with the same reaction.

When I raised my head, my eyes drifted over the vest, and I swear, I hardened even more.

"You like this?" I rasped, voice dark and wrecked. "Gettin' fucked in my cut? Bare and open? Ready to be bred?"

"Yes," Peyton cried. "Yes, yes, yes!"

I bent low, grabbing the back of her neck and crushing her mouth to mine as I pistoned into her, faster now, rougher. Each stroke hit deep, claiming her. Marking her. Fucking breeding her.

"You're gonna take my come," I grunted against her lips. "Gonna soak it up and make me a fuckin' daddy. You want that? Want me to knock you up?"

Her entire body locked, and her eyes flew wide. Her mouth opened, and all that came out was a raw, whimpering, "Yes."

That was it.

I pulled out and flipped her before she could blink, dragging her to her hands and knees with a growl. She gasped, hands bracing on the mattress, my name emblazoned on her back.

"This fucking view," I rasped, gripping her hips. "Seeing my patch while I fill you with my come."

She gasped, but she couldn't seem to form words anymore.

I shoved back in one hard thrust that made her cry out and bury her face in the sheets. Bending over her, I braced one hand beside her head, the other on her belly as I pounded into her.

"So fucking deep," I groaned in her ear. "Feel my cock claimin' you, baby?"

"I'm yours," she whispered as she shuddered and her walls fluttered around me.

"Fucking right. Now, you're gonna come for me," I growled. "While I'm buried in this tight little pussy, and then you're gonna milk my come like you fucking need it."

"Please," she cried out. "Please, Reid—"

I shoved a hand between her legs and pinched her clit. Her back bowed, and she screamed.

It was raw and perfect, her body locking up as her orgasm crashed into her. Pussy squeezing me tight, pulling me deeper, dragging me toward the edge with her.

"Oh fuck, yes, baby! Oh fuck! Fuck!"

I grabbed her hips, buried myself to the hilt, and let go.

A roar ripped from my throat as I came, hips jerking, seed spilling in her unprotected womb. I held her there, cock twitching inside her, fingers digging into her skin while I flooded her with every last drop.

When I was finally empty, I collapsed on top of her, panting like I'd just run a marathon. She trembled beneath me, boneless, flushed pink, and soaked in sweat.

I pulled out carefully, watching as my come leaked from her, thick and messy and...fuck, it was hot.

Before I passed out, I pulled her to the center of the bed with me, then gathered her close, hauling her against my chest and wrapping her in my arms like I'd never let her go.

She sighed, curling into me tighter. "I love you too, Reid."

My name on her lips did something to me. My heart felt like it was going to burst from my chest.

"I love you," I murmured against her hair, kissing her temple. "More than air. More than life."

I ran my hand down her back, feeling the soft

leather of the vest beneath my fingers. My patch, hugging her like a second skin.

And soon, my baby would be growing inside her.

Perfect.

Mine.

Always.

EPILOGUE
PEYTON

The summer heat clung to the air like a second skin, but I barely noticed it. Not when the ribbon was about to be cut on a project that had once been nothing more than an idea scrawled across the back of my college notebook. One that my husband had been determined to bring to life in only a few short months.

The brand-new children's library gleamed in the sun, the glass and stone façade reflecting the crowd that had gathered to celebrate its opening. Local news stations had shown up, a small stage had been assembled out front, and a huge banner fluttered overhead that read Welcome to Little Horizons Children's Library.

We hadn't been able to stop Reid's old crew

before they brought down the original building, but we'd raised enough money—and given our expertise —to make sure this one was even better.

I stood beside Reid, our fingers laced tightly together, the soft clink of our wedding rings audible whenever I adjusted my grip. His matching band glinted in the sun, a subtle contrast against the tattoo inked beneath it.

As soon as my finals were over, we got married in a ceremony that was loud, chaotic, beautiful—and very Iron Rogues. Fox had officiated. Gemma cried. Hawk's sister Sheridan caught the bouquet. My mom had come to town and never left. The only one who'd been missing was Racer because he'd been busy finding his old lady down in Florida.

Reid kissed me like he had no plans to stop. And I hadn't stopped smiling since.

Today, though, I was beaming for a different reason.

"You proud of me?" I murmured, leaning into Reid's side as applause echoed from the crowd. The mayor had just finished his speech, and the ceremonial scissors were being passed around behind us.

His arm tightened around my waist.

"Always. But today?" His mouth brushed my temple. "I'm fuckin' in awe, baby."

I looked up at him and laughed. "You're only saying that because you saw me wrangle that reporter into moving her truck out of the fire lane."

"That too." He smirked, then dropped his voice. "But mostly because I know exactly how hard you worked to make this happen."

He wasn't wrong. Between grant applications, community outreach, and chasing down contractors, it had been a marathon. But I wasn't alone. Reid had backed me every step of the way. So had the club. I'd never expected to find a family in a biker compound, but that was what I'd gotten.

And as of a few weeks ago, that family was growing. Something I had realized this morning.

My fingers twitched against Reid's. The secret I'd been keeping for the past few hours was already starting to feel too big to hold on to. But I was waiting for the perfect moment to share the news with him.

We watched the ribbon get sliced cleanly in two, cheers erupting from the crowd as the oversized scissors did their job. I caught sight of Dahlia wrangling her twins, same with Alice. Luna blew bubbles at her baby brother, with Molly and Maverick smiling at their antics.

My chest ached in the best way.

As the crowd began to filter toward the open doors, I felt a gentle nudge at my side.

"You okay?" Reid asked, watching me with a furrow in his brow.

"Yeah." I bit my lip. "More than okay."

We took a quick walk through the building, greeting guests and answering questions. I loved hearing the excited squeals from kids discovering the reading nooks and tech stations. The new library didn't just have books. It had classrooms, a 3D printer lab, and even a kitchen space for cooking classes. All built with reinforced safety measures, thanks to Reid's and my obsession with structural integrity.

When the crowd thinned out, Reid pulled me aside into a quiet corner of the library's staff office. He tilted my chin up and scanned my face. "You sure you're not overdoing it?"

I softened at the concern in his voice. "I swear I'm fine. Just a little tired."

He leaned in to kiss me, and I melted into him for a few seconds before I pulled back, a nervous flutter in my stomach.

"There's another reason I'm tired."

His expression turned serious instantly. "What is it?"

"It's early days yet, but apparently, it takes a lot of energy to grow a life."

His dark eyes widened when the meaning behind my words registered. "You tryin' to tell me that you're carrying my baby?"

"Yeah." I pressed his hand against my flat belly. "I just realized today how late my period is, so I took a test this morning."

"I'm so fucking happy." He captured my mouth in another deep kiss. "But next time, I'm there when you pee on that damn stick."

I gave him what he wanted every other time he knocked me up.

EPILOGUE
WRECKER

Our old farmhouse sat on ten acres on the west end of Old Bridge. The late afternoon sun stretched long shadows over the porch as the birds chirped in the trees. I'd gutted the whole place after we bought it—ripped out walls with my own hands, reinforced the frame myself, and built everything new from the bones out. Every nail, every board, every fucking hinge had my mark on it. I needed it that way. Needed to carve out a place in this world that was only *ours*.

A home.

Not just a place to sleep, but somewhere to belong.

I stood just inside the front door, filthy boots

planted wide on the scuffed hardwood and dust streaking my shirt while sweat clung to my back. But none of that shit mattered.

Because my attention was glued across the room. Peyton sat cross-legged on the couch, hair up in a loose, messy knot with a pencil stuck in it, flipping through one of her construction codes manuals. She had no clue I was watching her, and that made my desire for her even worse. Or better. Depending on how a man looked at it.

She was wearing my old tee—stretched across her tits and tight over her belly.

Perfect. My very pregnant, very fucking perfect woman.

Curled up next to her on the couch were our daughters, both fast asleep. Farrah had a blanket twisted around her legs and had a stuffed wolf tucked against her chest. Not quite two years old, and already a little spitfire. Just like her mom.

I was fucked the second she started talking in full sentences. Didn't stand a fucking chance. Learned that when our four-year-old, Mindy, opened her mouth and let out all her sass. She sighed in her sleep and snuggled her bear closer.

My girls were cute as fuck, and they had me wrapped around their little fingers.

A lump formed in my throat, and I scrubbed a hand down my face, swallowing hard as I crossed the room. Peyton looked up at the sound of my boots, and her whole face lit up, her smile cracking my chest open so my love poured out.

"You're home early," she whispered, voice soft so she wouldn't wake the girls.

"Yeah." My voice came out rougher than I meant, but I didn't care. I leaned down and kissed her, one hand sliding to her swollen belly like it had a magnetic pull. "Missed you."

She kissed me back, eyes closing, her lips soft and warm. "You always miss me."

"Fucking right I do."

I dropped to one knee in front of her, hands splaying over her stomach. When I felt the little kick against my palm, I grinned.

This one was a boy. *Thank fuck.* I needed backup with all these gorgeous girls to protect.

We found out last week. I'd nearly put my fist through the drywall in the clinic from the pressure of waiting even though I'd been good. I'd kept it together because Peyton wanted a calm moment.

And she'd gotten it.

Afterward, though...she didn't complain when I bent her over the bathroom sink and made sure she knew *exactly* how proud I was of what her body could do.

Now I rubbed a slow circle across her belly with my thumb and whispered low, "How's our boy?"

"He's restless. Been kicking the same spot since this morning."

Smirking, I leaned in and pressed a kiss right where she'd pointed. "That's my son. Already taking no shit."

Peyton laughed, shaking her head. "You're going to be impossible when he gets here."

"You knew that before you let me knock you up again, baby," I said, dragging my hand down her thigh. "Twice."

Her cheeks turned that pretty pink I never got tired of, and her violet eyes sparkled. "I did," she agreed. "And I'd do it all again."

I glanced at our daughters, still dead to the world, then cupped Peyton's jaw and kissed her long and slow. When I pulled back, her eyes were dazed and her lips slightly parted.

"Already done it again," I teased, patting her belly. "And if I get my way, it won't be the last time."

She snorted and shook her head. "You're relentless."

"And you fucking love me."

"I really do."

Sitting on the floor between her knees, I rested my head against her belly. She stroked my hair with one hand, her other curled around mine. Her skin was soft, her cinnamon and vanilla scent clinging to the air, mixing with sawdust and sunshine and the smell of home.

This was peace.

Not the kind I ever thought I'd get.

It was so much more than I could have imagined. The kind that made every rough thing worth it. Every nightmare, scar, and fucking hard-earned second that I spent with my family.

"You know what today is?" I asked quietly, eyes still shut.

"Hmm?"

"Five years since I pulled you out of that parking garage."

Peyton stilled, her fingers tightening in my hair.

I looked up, catching her soft gaze. "I didn't know it then, but that was the first moment I breathed *right*. The first moment I had something to fight *for*. Not just against."

She bit her lip, tears shining in her lashes. "You

always say the filthiest things...then ruin me with sweet stuff like that."

"Balance, baby." I chuckled and kissed her belly again. "I'm a fuckin' complicated man."

She snorted a laugh, and Mindy stirred slightly, murmuring something that sounded suspiciously like "Daddy."

Peyton smiled. "Looks like someone's waking up."

I stood slowly and scooped up our older girl, cradling her little body in my arms. She yawned, blinking up at me with those same violet eyes her mama had, sleep drunk and safe.

"You hungry, baby girl?"

She nodded, snuggling closer.

"Let's go raid the fridge," I murmured. "Mama and Farrah need rest."

Peyton grinned, watching me with love shining in her eyes.

And I knew, no matter what came next—what fires we had to walk through—I'd brave every single one just to see that look on her face.

I'd spent my life knocking shit down. But my woman, our family, this life, we'd built them together. And I wasn't ever fucking letting go.

Don't miss out on what happens when Racer finds the woman who's meant to be his down in Florida!

And if you join our newsletter, you'll get a FREE copy of The Virgin's Guardian, which was banned on Amazon.

ABOUT THE AUTHOR

The writing duo of Elle Christensen and Rochelle Paige team up under the Fiona Davenport pen name to bring you sexy, insta-love stories filled with alpha males. If you want a quick & dirty read with a guaranteed happily ever after, then give Fiona Davenport a try!

Printed in Dunstable, United Kingdom